PHILIPPA CAREY

THE THIRD SON

Complete and Unabridged

D1457710

LINFORD
ROMANCE

LINFORD
Leicester

First published in Great Britain in 2020

First Linford Edition
published 2022

Copyright © 2020 by DC Thomson & Co. Ltd.,
and Philippa Carey
All rights reserved

A catalogue record for this book is available
from the British Library.

ISBN 978-1-4448-4826-7

Published by
Ulverscroft Limited
Anstey, Leicestershire

Printed and bound in Great Britain by
TJ Books Ltd., Padstow, Cornwall

This book is printed on acid-free paper

THE THIRD SON

Lord Peter has disgraced the family once too often. Now his father is giving him one last chance to redeem himself. Go to the Devon estate and find out what is wrong with it: solve the problems, and the estate is his. Fail, and he will be cast off to make his own way in the world. Once in Devon, Lord Peter discovers resentful tenants, a thief, vicious smugglers — and, most significantly, a beautiful blind girl and her very clever dog . . .

Bleak Prospects

'I'm not going to give you another lecture on your behaviour,' the Marquess of Morton said to Peter, his youngest son. 'There's no point. You just go away and do whatever you want and now I have lost patience with you.

'This time the embarrassment to the family is too much and so I've decided on a different approach. Lady Day is next week and this,' he said, pointing to a small bundle of bank notes on his desk, 'is your allowance for the quarter. It is also your last allowance, for there will be no more after this one.'

Peter's eyebrows rose. This was indeed a new approach — and how, pray, was he expected to manage without an allowance?

'I will not pay any of your future debts and if you find yourself in debtor's prison it will be entirely your affair. So, you have three choices. Find yourself a rich heiress to marry in the next three months.

Find yourself employment. Or go to the Ermcombe estate in Devon and find out what is wrong with it.

'The income is negligible, whereas a few years ago it was nicely profitable. It's not entailed and if you manage to return it to profitability during the next quarter, I shall give it to you and then you will not need an allowance from me anyway.

'Fail to remedy whatever is wrong and I shall simply sell it. You can then do whatever you like, but without my help.'

This was an unexpected turn of events and Peter wasn't enthused by any of the alternatives. His father looked angry and determined, so he probably meant what he said.

His father stopped speaking and waited while his son mulled it over. Peter wasn't sure he knew many rich heiresses and he had no desire to marry in any case. Besides, his reputation probably meant there wasn't one who would be prepared to marry him, or rather, whose parents who would let him anywhere near their daughter.

He could take employment? But as what? A clerk or secretary? He could not imagine either alternative being to his liking. He had no desire to join the military like his older brother and knew he was unsuited to the clergy.

He doubted the East India Company would want him, although his father could probably persuade them, but he didn't fancy going to India anyway. So it was the estate. How hard could it be? He didn't really have any idea.

'I don't know anything about estate management.'

'No. I can see that was my mistake, but I never thought you would need to know with two older brothers. However, there is a steward down there to help you. Mind you, I don't know why he hasn't been able to make the estate profitable himself.

'There might be some unexpected sort of problem, so you may have to use your imagination to resolve it. Or if the steward is incompetent, I make you free to dismiss him and find a replacement.'

Whatever was wrong down in Devon, Peter could see he might need to be a fast learner, but surely it couldn't be too hard. He didn't know anything about turnips or mangel-wurzels (whatever they were) but there were tenant farmers to deal with this sort of thing, weren't there?

Presumably it was mostly a case of collecting the rents and if people didn't pay he could organise a bailiff to deal with them. Then, once the estate was profitable and providing him with an income to replace his allowance, he could return to his friends and clubs in London.

'Very well, I'll go to Devon. When should I leave?'

'Tomorrow. You have time to say goodbye to your mother and brothers. I'll send an express today to Ermcombe to warn them to expect you. I am supposing you will take your curricle and a riding horse.

'It should take you about three days to get there. You may write to me with what you find, but otherwise I shall not expect

4

to see you until the end of the quarter.'

He picked up the money and handed it to Peter, who thanked him, before turning to leave the study with no further word.

Peter was feeling shocked and bewildered by this surprising change in his circumstances. He trailed slowly upstairs towards his room. His only plans had been a dinner with his friends tomorrow and a trip to the spring races in Newmarket the following week. He would have to send a note to say he couldn't go to either.

He wondered if any of his friends might like a trip to Devon? Somehow he doubted it. He expected it to be very dull and no doubt they would, too. He sighed with resignation. He needed to tell his valet to pack and then go in search of his mother and brothers. He wasn't sure what reaction to his news he would get from any of them.

★ ★ ★

'Anne, we're going to take Sarah to London for the season. I'm afraid you will need to stay here. We don't want gentlemen imagining your blindness is hereditary and we won't get a chance to explain to them it was only because you got measles when you were a baby.

'Once Sarah is married, we will take you to London to see if we can find you a husband, but you shouldn't get your hopes up too much. I hope you understand why we have to do it this way.'

Anne was disconsolate, but she nodded. Yes, she did understand and she didn't want to blight her younger sister's chances of making a good match. Still, she would have liked to go to London. She might not have been able to dance at a ball, but at least she could have gone to musicales and concerts.

'I've written to your great-aunt Hermione to ask her to come and keep you company while we're away.'

Anne didn't mind Hermione; she wasn't the liveliest of people, but at least while Hermione was having a nap, Anne could do whatever she liked. Not that there was much she could do.

'Before you go, could we go into town to visit the bookshop?'

Anne's blindness meant they had found for her a well-spoken lady's maid called Mabel, the daughter of some tradespeople who had both died when she was only fourteen.

However, when she had been orphaned and looking for employment as a maid, she already knew how to read and write, so at least Anne could have books read to her while her family were away.

Both Mabel and Anne considered themselves lucky to have found each other and had become friends, as well as servant and mistress. Mabel also read and wrote the few letters which Anne sent and received.

'Of course. Perhaps this afternoon?'

'Yes, thank you. In the meantime I shall take Robbie for a walk.'

Robbie, her dog, had sat up upon hearing the word 'walk'. The dog had a saddle arrangement with a handle on top which the grooms had made for him. It meant Anne was able to reach down and grasp the handle without fumbling for a lead.

She could also feel which way Robbie was leading her. They headed for the door.

Once in the garden, Anne attempted to reconcile herself to being left behind. In truth, she had always known this would happen, but had tried not to think about it.

She wanted to have a husband and children, too, but she knew she might only ever be an aunt to her sister's children. An aunt who would never enjoy nephews and nieces properly if she couldn't see them or see what they were doing.

Would she ever have the chance to find a husband herself, a man she could love? The squire's son hinted from time to time how he wouldn't mind if his wife was blind, but this was hardly a good basis for marriage, especially when she was entirely indifferent to him.

No, it was more a case of him attempting a little social climbing.

She felt for edge of the bench in the rose garden and sat down. A cold breeze was wafting the smell of the roses towards her. She pulled her shawl around her shoulders, then scratched Robbie behind the ears. Robbie leant against her knee, hoping for more.

It was pleasant out here in the fresh air, despite the chill, but she felt sad about her poor prospects. It was going to be lonely here, even with Great Aunt Hermione, Mabel and Robbie.

At least when Mama was here and they had visitors, she could sit and listen to the conversation. Not that she got much chance to join in with the conversations, too many of the visitors equated blindness with simple-mindedness.

Anything she tried to contribute tended to be ignored. She doubted there would much chance to attend concerts in Plymouth either, since Hermione's hearing wasn't very good any more. It was going to be hard to bear, but at least she knew her sacrifice was to help her sister.

Courtesy Call

Peter's father was correct. It took him three days to reach the Ermcombe estate. There had seemed to Peter no point in racing down to Devon simply to embrace his fate.

As he drove into the entrance, he was surprised to see the gates standing wide with grass and weeds growing at the base.

He slowed down to take a good look. Clearly they had not been closed for some time. And where was the gate-keeper? The gatekeeper's cottage had dust and cobwebs in the windows. Was the estate so poor they could no longer afford one?

Peter kept his horses to a walk going down the drive to reduce the jolting of his curricle. The roadway was in bad repair, with weeds and ruts all the way along it.

He pulled to a halt at the steps leading up to the front door and looked around.

The front gardens needed a lot of attention, too. The grass didn't look as if it had been cut since the winter.

It occurred to him it was also much too quiet. Where was the groom running from the stables to take his horses? Why wasn't the butler standing at an open doorway?

Where were the footmen coming to collect his bags?

'Fredericks,' he said to his valet sitting beside him, 'unload the bags while I investigate what is going on.'

He jumped down, strode up to the front door, and pushed it open. The hallway was empty. Frowning, he stepped back and pulled the bell knob vigorously. He could hear the bell jangle in the distance.

After a short while, he could hear hurried footsteps on stairs and moments later a butler appeared at the far end of the hall, still buttoning his waistcoat. A footman followed him.

'I beg your pardon, my lord,' the butler said, 'but we were dining in the servants' hall. We didn't expect you until tomorrow at the earliest.'

Peter was tired, dusty, hungry and in no mood for apologies.

'Never mind that. Where are the grooms?'

'The groom was eating with us, my lord, he will be at the front at any moment. John,' he said, turning to the footman, 'get his lordship's bags.'

Peter frowned.

'The groom? Are you meaning to say there is only one groom, or did I misunderstand you?'

'No my lord, that is correct. Lord Morton gave directions to let all the grooms go, save one, since nobody from the family was in residence.'

Peter wondered, firstly, why his father hadn't mentioned this. Secondly, if there was a minimum of staff, why was the estate not profitable? It didn't take a genius or an expert in estate management to see a minimum of cost should result in a maximum of profit.

So why was it not the case? Lack of

staff would also explain the deplorable state of the drive.

'How many gardeners are there?'

The butler blinked. He obviously wasn't expecting this question.

'Just the one, sir — Johnson.'

It explained the drive, Peter thought. He was starting to wonder if his task here was going to be more difficult than he had supposed. However, questions about the other staff and the estate could wait until later.

'What is your name?'

'Richards, my lord,' the butler said with a slight narrowing of the eyes.

Peter realised he had made a slight faux pas. He had never thought to ask the names of the senior staff before he had left home. He didn't need or want to make friends of the servants, but antagonising them wouldn't help either. Oh well, he had much to learn.

'I would like to dine in a hour if it is feasible. Nothing large or complicated.'

'Very good, my lord, I will inform Cook,' Richards said with a slight bow.

'Is there still a housekeeper?'

'Yes, my lord,' a voice behind him said, 'I am Mrs Needham.'

He whirled to find a plump lady in black bombazine with keys at her waist curtseying to him.

'Shall I show you to your room, sir? I have already sent the girl up there with a can of hot water.'

Peter nodded and followed her upstairs, trailed by his valet and the footman carrying the bags. He thought about what she had said.

'You spoke of 'the girl'. Do I take it you have only one maid?'

'Yes, sir, this is correct.'

He didn't ask why, he was starting to get the general idea. Hopefully he would get a much better view of it all in the morning.

* * *

In the morning he sat down to a simple but satisfying breakfast. Rather than choosing from a range of dishes on the sideboard, he had simply been given a plate of eggs and bacon.

He realised it was an interesting change from the usual wide range of dishes, which he hardly ever touched. Dinner last night had been the same, but there was merit in simplicity.

'Richards,' he said, as he finished and stood up from the table, 'please show me where to find the study and then ask the steward to attend me.'

'Very good, sir, if you would follow me,' Richards said, 'the study is just down the hall. It has been cleaned and the decanters refreshed. I will send for the steward, Mr Smith, in just a moment.'

Peter went into the study and looked around. There was a desk, a couple of easy chairs and bookshelves, which were mostly empty.

Large windows opened on to the gardens at the back of the house, gardens which appeared to be as unkempt as those at the front. He was not now surprised in view of the shortage of staff in the house.

If he were to succeed in this endeavour, which appeared far from certain at present, the house and gardens would likely still be in a deplorable state by the end of the quarter.

He would have to hire a lot of staff to knock everything back into shape and would the estate be able to afford them?

He had visions of succeeding in winning the estate and then living as an old recluse in a tumbledown house. His grimaced at the idea his father might have given him a poisoned chalice. He wondered if it was deliberate or his father simply didn't know how things stood.

Ermcombe was the smallest of the Marquisate's many estates, and the most remote. Had he been sent here because it was the farthest away? Or because his father wasn't very interested in it? Peter realised the more he knew, the less he understood.

While Peter was still gazing gloomily at the wilderness of a garden, the door opened again and he turned around, expecting to meet the steward. Instead it was Richards again.

'My apologies, sir, but Mr Smith appears to be away from home.'

Peter's eyebrows rose. Everybody else knew of his arrival, so where was Smith? If the estate was in difficulties, surely he would have been here to explain how and where help was needed? If he was incompetent, his absence wasn't going to create a very good impression, was it?

'Do you know where he has gone or when he will be back?'

'No, sir,' Richards said dully, as if he neither knew nor cared.

Peter felt like cursing. Yet another unexpected wrinkle in his plans. A quarter sometimes seemed like a long time, but who knew what more bad surprises or delays he would come across? He really couldn't afford to waste a single day, because he was starting to think he would need as much time as possible.

In the meantime, what could he profitably do today? Riding around the estate or going through the books would be pointless without Smith to guide him.

'Who are the neighbours?'

'The closest neighbour is Baron Harford at the Harford estate. Beyond this are a large variety of small farms, mostly yeomanry, and then the town of Plymouth.

'Plymouth itself has a variety of various gentry, titled persons and naval officers.'

'Very well, I shall make use of my time with a courtesy call on Baron Harford. I suppose I am likely to find him at home?'

'Very likely, sir. He is married with two daughters and I have not heard of them travelling elsewhere.'

'Their ages?'

'Lord and Lady Harford must be about forty and their daughters perhaps twenty.'

Peter resisted the temptation to groan. At this point he did not need two diamonds distracting him nor two antidotes fawning all over him. He was probably going to be much too busy. Still, this was a necessary courtesy visit which, by convention, could at least be kept short.

'Very well. Ask for my riding horse to be brought around while I change into something suitable.'

★ ★ ★

An hour later he rode up to a substantial, but modestly styled, red brick house of Georgian design. He couldn't help but notice it was all neat, tidy and had pretty gardens, in contrast to the Ermcombe house. This place was properly organised, too, he thought, as a groom came sprinting around from the stables.

'I don't expect to be long,' Peter said, tossing the reins to the groom. 'Just give him a drink if he wants one.'

The groom raised a finger to his brow and led the horse away as Peter went to the door. The door was opened quickly to his knock by a butler whose glance rapidly assessed the caller as a gentleman, and the door was opened wide.

'Is the baron at home?' Peter asked, offering his card.

'I will ascertain, sir, if you would be

good enough to wait here a moment,' the butler said, taking the card and placing it on a salver, before pacing away into the house.

Moments later a slightly portly gentleman came back down the hall, followed by the butler. It was clearly the baron himself, who had a smiling, somewhat chubby face and a full head of black hair, although it was starting to recede. He shook Peter's hand vigorously.

'Lord Peter, how good of you to call. I am Harford. Please come up to the drawing-room so I can introduce you to my family. We had heard you would be arriving, but did not anticipate seeing you quite so soon.'

Peter wondered if arriving later than intended or expected was a commonplace in this part of the country. Possibly something to do with the deplorable state of the roads?

They went upstairs slowly, following the butler.

'Do you intend to be here for long?' Harford asked.

'At least until the end of the quarter.'

'Oh, an extended visit, then?'

'Yes, my father has asked me to come and see what is wrong with the estate. So far, it looks a bit run down.'

'Indeed, I've had one of my tenants complaining about weed seeds blowing on to his land, but your steward was either not inclined or not able to do anything about it.'

'I have yet to see the steward as he is away from home, but I shall certainly quiz him about it when he appears.'

They approached the drawing-room doors, behind which they were sounds of feverish activity. It all went quiet as the butler opened the doors and announced Peter. As he entered he saw there were three ladies standing to great him.

'May I introduce Lady Harford, and my daughters Miss Anne and Miss Sarah.'

Peter bowed to them and the ladies curtseyed in return. As they did so, he caught sight of the younger daughter elbowing the elder, as if she needed urging to make her curtsey.

'We are pleased to meet you, my lord,' Lady Harford said. 'We have been looking forward to making your acquaintance, haven't we, girls?'

'The pleasure is all mine.'

As they exchanged polite expressions, they were all making quick assessments and first impressions of each other. Peter saw Lady Harford was becomingly a little portly, rather like her husband. The elder daughter was slim, with shining hair, and she struck him as remarkably pretty. Her younger sister was passably pretty too and had auburn hair the same shade as that of her mother.

Peter marked the baron as straightforward, his wife was looking decidedly smug, the younger daughter looked as if she was about to simper and the elder . . . the elder had a certain vagueness about her.

Her sister was looking at him admiringly, but the elder was gazing over his shoulder in an unfocused way. Was she a little simple-minded? Was this why she had needed a prompt before curtseying?

'I do hope you will dine with us one evening,' Lady Harford said.

'I shall be pleased to do so,' Peter replied. 'However, I would beg you to keep it restrained and ordinary. As the son of a marquess I am always presented with a large number of very complicated dishes.

'In the last few days I have come to realise my palate has become quite jaded and I am finding a few plain dishes, well prepared, have been much more enjoyable.'

He thought his potential hostess looked a little dismayed. Perhaps she had been hoping to impress her social superior with the prowess of her chef? The daughter Sarah looked a little puzzled and her elder sister had a small smile on her face. Their father looked pleased. Peter wondered if he would understand this family better after meeting them in future, as was inevitable.

'Will you be going up to London for the season, milord?' Sarah asked.

'I'm afraid not,' he said. 'I'm sure I will have too much to do here in Devon up until midsummer day. Beyond this I cannot be sure.'

Peter knew he wouldn't be able to afford staying in London during the coming season and beyond this, who could guess? For all he knew, he might be heading to America to seek his fortune. It wasn't something he wanted to explain to new neighbours.

Sarah was rather obviously trying not to pout. Her sister looked faintly surprised. Their mother looked even more dismayed.

Presumably she had been hoping Lord Peter, their new acquaintance, would have been able to gain them entrance to some of the more select events of the season.

Unfortunately, there was very little Peter could do about it. He supposed he could write a letter of introduction, but his current reputation was such it might do more harm than good.

Perhaps his father might condescend

to them a little if he thought befriending a respectable family was a start to his son's redemption. Besides, they were, in a sense, his neighbours.

'I shall be writing to my father in a few days' time and I shall mention your names. No doubt he will be pleased to see you if he is in London during the season.'

Peter had no idea if his father would be there, nor if he would be pleased or not, but it was the only olive branch he could offer.

'In the meantime, I must be going as I have much to do,' he said, remaining standing.

He bent over Lady Harford's hand, who was now looking more cheerful. Miss Sarah held out her hand so he was obliged to bend over it too. Her sister stood as well, but didn't hold out her hand, so he merely bowed to her and followed their father out of the room.

'I should perhaps have said before,' the baron said as they went downstairs, 'but Anne, my eldest, is blind. She contracted measles when she was a baby and has been blind since then.

'Older children can usually shrug off the effects of the disease, but Anne was unluckily very young at the time, and there is nothing to be done now. Still, she knows her way around the house and gardens and we do what we can.'

Everything now became clear to Peter. The girl wasn't simple at all, she just couldn't see what was going on. He felt guilty at the way he had totally misjudged her. She had known when he was about to leave, but had not known to offer her hand like her sister.

In any case, her sister had been a little presumptuous, but this was another matter. It also explained why she had appeared to be gazing in a vague way over his shoulder. He determined to engage her in conversation next time they met.

'You said you expected to be busy,' the baron said, 'is it your intention to set the estate to rights?'

'Yes, it is, but frankly, I'm not sure where to begin, or how. With two older brothers, I never thought I would need to know. It is a great nuisance the steward is away and nobody seems to know where he is or when he will be back.'

'If I can be of assistance, do not hesitate to ask. We shall be going up to London in a week or ten days, so be sure to come before then and not just for dinner.'

They shook hands at the door.

'Thank you, Harford, I'm sure I will.'

Alarming Discovery

'What is he like?' Anne asked.

'Oh, he is very handsome,' Sarah said with a sigh. 'He is tall and wide of shoulder. His hair is dark brown and curly. His face looks strong and manly, too. I do hope there will be men like him in London for me to dance with.'

'I liked the sound of his voice,' Anne said, 'but I expect Mama was disappointed he only wanted a plain dinner!'

'Well, yes, I was,' her mother admitted, 'but I expect what is plain for the son of a marquess is not what we would consider plain. However, I suppose we must be a little restrained.

'Nevertheless, I expect we shall have many turtle dinners in London and Sarah will have many handsome dancing partners, too. I have to say Lord Peter was very gentlemanly and it was gratifying he came to visit us so promptly.'

Anne thought her mother sounded very pleased with the visit. She hoped they would not be disappointed in London. At least if they had an introduction to the marquess, they might receive invitations elsewhere as a result. With a bit of luck, the marquess would not be too high in the instep to mention their name around. After all, his son seemed happy enough to visit her father, who was a mere baron. It was important to become known in London, otherwise they were likely to spend a lot of time at home.

Anne wondered if Lord Peter had brothers who were not married. After all, Sarah was said to be pretty although a marquess's heir was surely above her touch. Still, there was no knowing to whom she might appeal. In the meantime they had an interesting neighbour.

She hoped he would visit again and not just once for dinner. It might relieve the inevitable boredom of the summer to come.

★　★　★

On his gentle ride back to Ermcombe, Peter wondered what to do with the rest of his day, assuming Smith hadn't reappeared in the meantime. He decided to look around the stables. There was a lot about estates and farms he didn't understand, but this didn't include horses and stables.

Accordingly, when he reached home he rode into the stable yard, rather than leave his horse at the front door.

As he clattered into the cobbled yard, the groom emerged to take his horse. Dismounting, Peter looked around. It was reasonably tidy, although there were a few weeds here and there in the corners. If there was only the one groom, he was probably doing as well as could be expected.

'How many horses are there?'

'Well, sir, there be your pair from your curricle and this'n. Then there be the cob what is used for the gig an' Mr Smith's riding horse, except he ain't here right now. Then sometimes there'll be the horses from the traders, but o'course thems only here for a few hours.'

'Traders?'

'The traders what come to see Mr Smith.'

Peter wasn't sure who these traders were or why they visited, but Smith could tell him when he got back.

'Speaking of Smith, do you know where he's gone?'

The groom frowned as he slowly thought it over.

'Nay, can't say as I do, sir. Looked like he might be goin' away for quite a while though.'

'Gone for a while? Why do you say so?'

'Well, on account of him having two big bags either side o' his saddle and another big satchel over his shoulder.'

A suspicion was forming in Peter's mind.

'Where does he live?'

The groom pointed towards the back of the house.

'One o' them cottages out back. One's Johnson's, the head gardener's, t'other be Smith's.'

Peter left the groom to stable his horse and walked around to the back of the house. The cottages were set away from the main house, shielded by a row of trees, but not difficult to find. There were rows of vegetables in front of them, currently being weeded by an old man.

'Are you Johnson?'

'Aye, my lord,' the old man said, straightening up slowly, as if he had backache.

'Which one of these cottages is Smith's?'

'The one on the left, sir, the other one is mine.'

Peter nodded, and strode towards Smith's cottage, Johnson watching him as he went.

'You'll not find him home, sir,' Johnson called.

Peter waved acknowledgement of the information. He already knew Smith wasn't there and he had a suspicion Smith wasn't going to be coming back either.

He open the unlocked door and went

in. It was cold and somehow it felt unoccupied, too. He went through to the room at the back. On the table was a small piece of bread which felt stale. Next to it was an unwashed mug and plate.

He climbed a ladder to the attic where there was an unmade bed and little else, except for an old pair of muddy boots tossed to the side. He needed no further convincing. Smith was gone and not coming back. The question was, why?

It was a question he mulled over while he had a lunch of bread, ham and ale. Had Smith expected to be sacked for incompetence and decided to leave first?

No, there was no point in doing so. He might have been able to hope for a severance gift. Then, by all accounts, he had told nobody where he was going. Had he been offered a better post elsewhere? No, there was no sense in the whole affair. Perhaps the estate records would offer a clue.

'Richards,' he said as soon as he finished eating, 'show me to the estate office, would you?'

'Yes, sir, it is downstairs near the housekeeper's room and my pantry.'

Peter followed him down into the servants' area and along the plain corridor to the estate office. He paused at the entrance. There were shelves full of box files and ledgers. Every flat surface was covered by piles of documents. He was dismayed. He had no idea where to start or even what he was looking for.

After surveying it all for several minutes, he realised he needed help and also the best place in which to find it. It was humiliating, but he needed to go straight back and throw himself on the mercy of his neighbour. Harford would no doubt be surprised to see him back so soon, but after all, he had said not to hesitate or delay asking for help.

'Richards, have my horse brought around to the front again, if you please.'

It was just as well he hadn't changed out of his riding clothes.

★ ★ ★

A short while later he was once more trotting up the front of Harford House. This time he could see Anne standing at the front, holding a harness of some sort on a black and white dog and apparently listening to the sound his horse was making on the gravel drive.

'Good afternoon, Miss Harford,' he said loudly, to be sure she could hear him clearly.

'Lord Peter,' she said, smiling in his direction. Obviously she recognised his voice from earlier.

He dismounted and dropped the reins, his horse sufficiently well trained to simply stand there quietly.

'You may let go of the dog,' he said, 'my horse is accustomed to dogs as am I, so there is no need to hold him back.'

She laughed.

'Oh, no, my lord, you don't understand. This is my dog, Robbie, he is my helper. I keep hold of him so he may guide me around obstacles. It would never do for me to trip and fall in the fountain, would it?'

'Indeed it would not, but I have never heard of such a dog. May I say hello to him?'

'Yes, of course you may, he's very friendly.'

Peter approached them and crouched down, before offering the back of his hand to be smelled. Robbie obligingly sniffed his hand before giving it a lick.

'I think he approves of you,' she said, 'I can hear his tail wagging on the gravel.'

'He is certainly a very handsome dog,' Peter said, straightening up and thinking the dog's mistress was handsome, too. When she smiled, her whole face lit up and then she was exceedingly pretty. But this was not something he could remark upon, especially at such a short acquaintance.

However, he felt he might like to get to know her better. He would have to make a point of visiting here again before they all went to London.

'How did you come by such a dog?'

'I wanted a dog to keep me company, and when the shepherd was asked for a suitable dog, he said he thought he could train it to be useful, too. After all, he trains his own dogs to herd the sheep.

'He trained Robbie to guide me so I don't walk into things or lose my way. Robbie certainly gives me more freedom than I would otherwise have.'

'I would be interested to see how he helps you, but I'm afraid it must be another day. In the meantime I need to consult your father on a matter of business.'

'Of course, I would be glad to show you how clever Robbie is when you have time to spare. I don't have a great deal of company and visitors are always welcome.'

He fell in beside her, on the opposite side from Robbie, as they headed towards the front door and a groom led his horse away. He thought she sounded lonely.

'Would you ring the bell?' she asked, 'or simply open the door for us?'

Peter did both, as he wasn't sure of the etiquette for a situation like this.

As they entered, the butler came to hold the door open.

'Good afternoon, my lord,' he said, standing to one side so as not to obstruct Anne and Robbie. He didn't seem surprised Peter was back so soon. Perhaps he had remarkable foresight or was merely unflappable.

'Would you ask Lord Harford if he could spare me a few minutes of his time?'

Anne nudged a chair in the hallway before taking a seat, Robbie sat beside her.

'My mother and sister have gone into Plymouth,' she said, 'to buy new hats. Mother is determined to arrive in London in the latest style.

'I cannot help but wonder if hats made in Plymouth will be seen as in the latest style in London. What do you think, my lord?'

She smiled up at him. Peter was taken aback. Was she joking or serious? He realised he didn't know her well enough to tell. Furthermore, whatever answer he gave, it was ripe for misinterpretation and the giving of offence. Was she testing him in some way?

'I really could not say, Miss Harford, I am far from being an expert on ladies' fashions in hats. But did you not want to go with them into Plymouth?'

'To what purpose? I am unable to see the difference between one hat and another, am I? Besides, I am not going to London.'

Peter could not mistake a small amount of bitterness in her voice. He couldn't tell if it was the inability to choose a hat or of not going to London. She sounded wistful, too. Surely her mother could choose a nice hat for her, so . . .

'Why are you not going to London?'

'If gentlemen think blindness runs in the family, suitors for my sister's hand will be frightened away, so it is best if I remain here.'

Peter was incensed. Had her family no feelings or sensitivity?

'The cause of your blindness is no secret, and if this is sufficient to frighten men away, then they are stupid and you are all well rid of them. They would do better to realise beauty runs in your family and how it is rather more to the point.'

A smile spread across her face, but he didn't notice as he had turned to face the returning butler.

'His lordship will see you now, sir.'

'Thank you,' he said to the butler. He turned back to Anne.

'Until next time, Miss Harford. I shall look forward to a demonstration of Robbie's talents in the near future.'

Help is at Hand

Anne thought about their encounter as she sat in the entrance hall. She hadn't expected to meet Peter again until he came for dinner, but she was glad he had returned so soon. She didn't know why he needed to speak with Father, but it did suggest he wasn't planning to keep his distance from Harford House.

If only Peter would visit when the family had gone to London it would relieve the tedium. It seemed he liked dogs and Robbie liked him as well, which was pleasing.

He spoke to her as if she was a real person, too, not as if she was a simpleton. He even seemed angry for her sake when he heard she wasn't being taken to London.

Unfortunately this might mean he was only being polite about meeting her again if he had expected her to go. And he had said beauty ran in her family.

Anne hugged the thought to herself.

He hadn't said it flirtatiously, either; in fact, he sounded irritated at the way some men might be frightened away by her blindness. He had said it without thinking and as if he really meant it.

She knew Sarah was considered pretty, but did this mean Peter thought she, Anne, was pretty, too? As well, he had promised to come again and see how clever Robbie was. She was a bit confused by their chance meeting.

Whatever happened, Anne felt happy to have received some attention from a gentleman whom her sister had described as handsome, no matter it could never come to anything more.

* * *

'I hadn't expected to see you again quite so soon,' the baron said, as Peter entered his study. 'Please take a seat and tell me how I can help you?'

'Not to beat about the bush, I have come to throw myself upon your mercy. I should perhaps begin at the beginning and tell you the whole story and trust you will keep the details confidential.'

The baron nodded.

'Of course.'

'I was in disgrace with my father. As a third son, unsuited to the military or the clergy, I was unsuited to anything else either, except a hedonistic lifestyle, but I went too far. My father cast me off except for sending me down here to find out what is wrong with the Ermcombe estate.

'If I can use my initiative and restore the estate to what it should be, he will make me a gift of it with the consequent independence. If I fail, I will have nothing at all.

'Obviously I have a powerful incentive to put the estate back into good order, but frankly, I know nothing about estate management. I came down here expecting I could learn whatever I needed from the steward, even if he was incompetent.

'Then, perhaps using a little imagination, I had hoped to put it all to rights.

Instead, I discover the steward has absconded. Nobody knows where he has gone and I expect this was his intention.

'Since there was nothing to be gained from leaving before he was dismissed, I am therefore speculating he has left with more in his pockets than he was entitled to.

'The problem is, I know nothing and I have no idea even where to begin. I am hoping you or your steward might be able to give me some pointers on where I should start and what I should do.'

The baron sat back in his chair as he contemplated the situation and his new neighbour's predicament.

'Well. I see. It is a difficult situation to be in. You have been very candid. I admire you for admitting it and not being too proud to seek help. Rest assured, I will do whatever I can to assist you.

'However, my wife is dragging me off to London in a matter of days, so I may not be able to do much more than get you started.

'Davis, my steward, has gone into

Plymouth on an errand this afternoon, but we will call on you first thing tomorrow to look into it. I will ask him to provide whatever assistance he can while I am away as well.

'In all probability you will need to visit an agency in Plymouth the day after tomorrow to see if they know of a suitable replacement. Does your father have a deputy steward he could lend you in the meantime?'

'He may. I don't know and I had no reason to ask before. I hope my father will agree to assist me, but in any case it will take four or five days for a letter to reach him and for somebody to come in the opposite direction.

'My father has given me until the end of the quarter which is about to start, so I don't feel I have any time to waste. I have to say I am very grateful for your willingness to help me in the meantime.'

'It is in nobody's interest to have Ermcombe neglected and I am happy to provide whatever assistance I may.

Hopefully my daughter Sarah will find

herself a husband promptly and then we can come home.

'I don't care for the dirt and smells of London, I much prefer the fresh air which blows here from the sea. In the meantime, I shall tell Davis to render you whatever assistance he can.'

'Your daughter doesn't aspire to one of the admirals in Plymouth?'

'Goodness no, my wife wouldn't allow it. She is determined Sarah shall find herself a title, and thus we must go to London. Personally, I couldn't care less if there is a title or not, as long as Sarah is happy with whomsoever she finds.'

Peter reflected, with a small amount of relief, how he seemed to be out of the running. Marriage was far from his thoughts just at the moment too and he was happy not to be pursued by hopeful mothers and daughters. Sorting out the Ermcombe estate was quite enough to keep him occupied.

★　★　★

The next day, Friday, the baron and his steward arrived at Ermcombe House soon after breakfast. Richards conducted them, and Peter, down to the steward's office.

Baron Harford and Davis paused just inside the entrance to the office.

'Not as neat and tidy as your office, is it?' the baron commented to his steward.

'No, sir,' Davis said, 'and it does look as if it has been left rather hurriedly.'

He turned to Peter.

'My lord, did Smith act as both land and house steward?'

'I believe so,' Peter said, tacitly admitting his ignorance. He glanced at Richards who nodded agreement.

Davis went across to the large desk and examined two ledgers left carelessly on top of various papers. He leafed through one to the page holding the latest entries, then took the other and did the same. He compared one with the other.

'Mr Richards, might I ask how much you are paid?' Davis asked.

Richards looked at Peter, who nodded

for Richards to answer.

'Thirty pounds per year, naturally plus bed and board.'

Davis pointed to an entry in one ledger. Peter leaned closer and saw it was the sum entered in the book.

Peter wasn't at all knowledgeable about servants' wages, but it didn't seem very much to him as the pay for a butler.

'Harford, how much is Mr Gerrard, your butler, paid?' he asked.

'I think it is sixty pounds a year, which is quite a difference, isn't it?'

'It is indeed,' Peter said, frowning and glancing at Richards, 'and it doesn't seem right.'

'This is not all,' Davis said, 'the second ledger has similar entries but for quite different amounts.' He pointed to an entry in the second ledger.

'Eighty pounds?' Peter said, not understanding what he was looking at.

'Yes, this ledger shows Mr Richards as being paid eighty pounds a year. It is my guess,' Davis said, 'the first ledger shows what was actually paid and the second

48

ledger is what was reported to Lord Morton.'

They all looked at each other as they considered the implication.

'So are you suggesting the difference of fifty pounds found its way into Smith's pocket?'

'This would be a simple explanation, yes.'

'Richards, would you fetch Mrs Needham, please?'

If the butler was being cheated, then in all probability the housekeeper and all the other servants were being cheated too.

Comparisons between the two ledgers showed similar tales for all the other servants. It was becoming clear why Smith had decided to leave in a hurry when he heard Lord Peter was on his way.

Peter was angry, but realised pursuit was a waste of time. It would not surprise him if Smith had headed to the nearby Plymouth and taken the first ship going to America.

He probably had pockets plump with

stolen money sufficient to start a new and prosperous life on the other side of the Atlantic. At least Peter now had an inkling of why the estate was in such a mess.

'It appears Smith has been robbing all the servants and my father, too,' Peter said. 'I can see little point in a hue and cry, as he is probably on board ship in mid-Atlantic at this point.

'However, Richards, I can do something about the servants' pay. Next Monday is the quarter day and you may inform all the servants they will receive the proper amount they should have been earning. I think halfway between what was actually paid and what was reported to my father is probably about right.'

Peter noticed Richards and Mrs Needham glance at each other. They looked not only surprised, but pleased, too. This was a change from the stony faces he had seen up until now. If they had thought his father was deliberately paying them badly, it was not surprising if they had resented his son's presence on some sort of visit of inspection.

'Why would Smith keep two ledgers, thus revealing what he had been doing?' Peter asked Davis.

'The problem with lies is remembering how you lied previously. Inconsistency would have raised suspicions. In this case he appears to have had an escape already planned before his thefts could be discovered. He might not have cared we knew what he had been doing if, by then, he was far away.'

'At least it has made it easy for us to understand what has been happening.'

'Might I suggest we find the ledgers for rents paid by the tenant farmers and also the record of payments to tradesmen?' Davis said.

'Yes, indeed. It would be surprising if Smith had not taken the opportunity to rob everybody else too,' a resigned Peter said.

It was fortunate his father had given him his allowance for the forthcoming quarter and he had spent very little of it.

It would be enough to pay the servants on Monday. It was unlikely there was any money in the house and who knew what the rents would provide?

Harford, Davis and Peter soon found the tenant farmers were being charged three times the amount reported to the marquess.

'I see now,' Peter said, 'why my father thought the estate was doing barely better than break even. I need to write to him, explain what was going on and beg the assistance of one of his stewards or men of business.

'After luncheon I shall visit the farmers and tell them how they have been robbed. I am grateful, Davis, for the way you have revealed so quickly what has been going on.'

'It would have been more difficult and taken longer had Smith taken the time to cover things up. As it is, he appears to have dropped everything and departed.'

'Have you looked for a strong box or safe?' the baron asked.

'I haven't, but I shall not hold my

breath, as I'm sure they will be empty.'

'Yes, I doubt there will be any money, but there could be important documents such as deeds to the property.'

'True. I must make a tour of the house and see if anything else is missing. He may have sold pictures, for example, but I don't believe there are any family portraits or paintings by famed artists.'

'Speaking of family, I have been told to invite you to dinner tomorrow. Thank heavens I didn't forget, otherwise my wife would have had my guts for garters.'

Lost in Admiration

'Good evening, Lord Peter,' the baron said, as Peter entered the drawing-room at Harford House.

'Good evening, Harford,' Peter replied with a smile, as he shook the baron's hand. 'And good evening, Lady Harford. Thank you for your invitation. No doubt Lord Harford has appraised you of our discoveries yesterday.'

'Yes, he has and we were quite shocked by what was discovered.'

'It is the punishment for neglect of the estate, I am afraid. I am hoping it may all be rectified in short order.'

Peter moved to be in front of Anne. He bowed, even though he knew she couldn't see him. She surprised him a little by an answering curtsey. Clearly she had realised he was in front of her. He wondered if she had heard his clothes rustle, heard his shoes on the parquet floor or merely assumed he would bow to her next. In any case, he was unreasonably pleased.

'Miss Harford, I hope I find you well. I look forward to hearing more about Robbie as soon as there is an opportunity. He is not with you this evening?'

'No, my lord, he is off duty and downstairs eating his own dinner.'

'In that case, I hope to renew his acquaintance some other day.'

Peter was pleased to find he had prompted a small smile from her. He moved on to her sister.

'Miss Sarah, good evening,' he said with a bow.

'Good evening, my lord,' she replied with a curtsey. As she rose, she looked at him coyly through her eyelashes. This was a trick familiar to him, but he was unmoved. She didn't interest him any more than dozens of young ladies he had met before.

Her father appeared at Peter's shoulder and indicated an older lady who had remained seated.

'May I introduce you to my aunt, Lady Hermione, the Dowager Countess Danvers. Aunt Hermione, this is our new neighbour Lord Peter Wilson.'

He made another, deeper, bow to her and received merely a nod in return.

'Good evening, Lady Hermione, I am pleased to meet you. Am I correct in thinking you are a friend of my grandmother, the Dowager Marchioness?'

'Exactly so, young man,' she said with a frown, 'she has told me a great deal about you. I was a little surprised to hear from Harford you were down here in Devon and not still racketing about like a wild thing in London.'

Ah, Peter thought, she knew of his reputation and was not shy of a little blunt speaking. Thank goodness he had remembered who she was, otherwise she would surely have been offended. It would not help his task in Devon if he was known as a fribble. If he was to gain the estate at the end of the quarter, he needed people to take him seriously.

'Unfortunately, it was a consequence of being a third son with little purpose in life. Now you see before you, ma'am, a reformed character. I am here to learn estate management and become a respectable landowner.'

She snorted her disbelief.

'So Morton boxed your ears and sent you here for something useful to do, did he?' Lady Hermione nodded her understanding.

Peter winced. This lady saw too much.

'Well, we shall see how you get on,' she continued. 'I shall be here for the next few months as companion to my great-niece Anne whilst the others go gallivanting off to London and get Sarah riveted to someone respectable. You need not make any suggestions in that regard, I doubt you know anyone suitable.' She sniffed and looked away, clearly dismissing him, now he had been put in his place.

'My lords, ladies, dinner is served,' Gerrard the butler intoned.

Anne had heard the slight sound of Peter moving in front of her when he had finished speaking with her mother. When he spoke to her, there was warmth in his voice and she was pleased he remembered Robbie. It was nice to be greeted in a personal way, rather than being dismissed out of hand as happened with some visitors.

She was then interested to note his interaction with Sarah was only a brief courtesy. Sarah, the pretty one, was usually the one who attracted all of a gentleman's attention. For some reason he must be unimpressed by her sister.

The exchange with Great-aunt Hermione was even more fascinating to Anne. Peter had seemed to be a complete gentleman, polite, respectful and thoughtful. Yet, to hear Aunt Hermione, he was disgraceful, had been living a wild life in London and was sent here as some sort of punishment. He even admitted it. Was his charm just a facade?

Perhaps she should be a bit wary of him and take care not to be deceived into anything foolish.

When they reached the dining-room, Peter was relieved to realise Lady Hermione would sit on Harford's right and he would sit on Lady Harford's right.

As he was diagonally across from Lady Hermione, he was confident she would not break with convention by sending him verbal barbs across the table.

He was then pleased to find Anne on his right, with whom he could converse, and across the table from Sarah, with whom he could not converse without incurring the wrath of Lady Hermione.

This did not stop Sarah from fluttering her lashes at him, which he pretended not to notice. Clearly Sarah was not concerned by his reputation, but since she was going to London and he wasn't, she probably didn't care. He wondered what Anne thought of it all.

He also wondered and worried how Anne would manage at the dining table, considering she couldn't see the food in front of her. He hoped, for her sake, nothing would go wrong to embarrass her when they had visitors.

The first course was soup which was served to her by Gerrard himself. Peter observed, from the corner of his eye, how she felt the position of the plate and then the spoon, after which there was no difficulty.

For the next course, everyone, except Anne, served themselves from dishes held by the footmen. Again, Gerrard served Anne himself, before whispering in her ear. Having spent the first course talking to her mother, politeness now required he speak to Anne on his other side.

'Did you enjoy the fish soup, my lord?' she asked.

'Yes, indeed, it was excellent. I imagine it is a benefit of living so close to the sea.'

'Our cook has become quite skilled at making many different fish dishes.'

'Forgive me, Miss Harford, but I am going to be rude and impertinent, and if you reprimand me, I shall be penitent and bite my tongue. However, I am compelled by curiosity. The soup course was straightforward, but how will you manage with the food on your plate now when you cannot see it?'

'Ah,' Anne said with a smile, 'Gerrard places food on my plate in a precise manner. So, for example, he will place pieces of chicken on my plate and whisper to me there is chicken at twelve o'clock. Then he will tell me there are green beans at three o'clock, and so on. Once I know what to expect where, I can do the rest by touch with my knife and fork. Observe my plate, my lord.'

Peter looked down and saw what she meant, there was food arranged around the plate, just as she had described.

'What an ingenious method! Had you not told me, I would probably not have realised how it was done.'

'Furthermore, the cutlery and wine glasses are in exactly the same position every time, so I know where to find everything. But a good butler and his staff should be laying the table this way for everyone, anyway, should he not?'

'I agree, but to be honest, I had never thought about it before.'

Peter saw this was something, probably one of a number of details, he had never even noticed before.

'I am beginning to realise, Miss Harford, there are a great many things I have taken for granted in the past. Now I no longer have ready access to great wealth, hordes of servants and a well-run house, I am feeling rather chastened by my lack of knowledge.

'Ermcombe is a small, rather run-down estate without many servants, so I am already having to modify my expectations. I am finding it very educational. Forgive me if I am indelicate, but now I am even appreciating how much I should be grateful for the gift of sight.'

'Sometimes, my lord, you have to make an adjustment for what you have, be grateful for it, and not weep over what you do not have.'

'Your strength and wisdom humbles me, Miss Harford. I am lost in admiration.'

'Now, now, sir, no flattery if you please. Great Aunt Hermione has warned us innocent young girls to be on our guard against hardened rakes such as yourself.'

Peter's eyes flicked across to where the lady in question was talking to his host. He had not anticipated coming across such a tough critic in the depths of Devon.

'Ah, yes. She has already made it clear she has an extremely poor opinion of me. I shall have my work cut out to make myself respectable.'

Anne had indeed been warned by Great-aunt Hermione not to be taken in by a persuasive libertine who was no doubt an experienced charmer. All the same, she was enjoying Peter's company. Was he being merely flattering in the way he was talking to her and enquiring about how she managed?

She thought he seemed genuinely interested. He also sounded more honest and open than she had expected. She certainly hadn't expected him to be frank about a wild past, although she wasn't clear exactly what this might have involved.

Presumably there was no point in denying it with a bold critic like Great-aunt Hermione in the room.

Once they had reassembled in the drawing-room after dinner, Anne took her place at the piano. Peter was impressed by the standard of Anne's playing. He was also filled with admiration because not only was the piece played well, but it was obviously done from memory. At the end they all applauded loudly.

'Harford, your daughter is very talented. I am astonished she plays so well and without the benefit of the music in front of her.'

'We have a music teacher who comes a couple of times a week. It is the least we can do in the circumstances and then she practises for hours, too. She deserves our applause simply for the amount of hard work she does.'

Sarah moved to the piano and started sorting some sheet music.

'Sarah has the teacher, too,' the baron continued, 'but she doesn't have the same application and determination. Of course, as she has many other things she can do, she doesn't have the same motivation.'

'Does she excel at something else then?'

'Her watercolours are good and she has a fair seat on a horse.'

'Anne does not ride?'

'No. It's not very interesting to simply sit on a horse and have someone else lead you. She said she didn't want to bother to learn because it was just as interesting to sit in an open carriage and it was less tiring, too.'

★　★　★

As he cantered home in the moonlight, Peter reflected upon his evening. He felt some sympathy for the elder daughter. Anne had a major disadvantage, but she tried not to let it hold her back. Despite her efforts, he felt perhaps her family could sometimes be kinder; not that he thought they were being deliberately unkind.

When her mother and sister had gone into Plymouth to buy new hats, why hadn't they taken Anne, too? Surely any young girl would like a new hat? Did it matter she wouldn't be able to see it and wasn't going to London to wear it? She could feel the hat, be told it was becoming and feel pretty when she wore it, even if it was only to church.

He wondered if he could take her to buy a new hat himself. Of course, it would be most improper unless he took her dragon of a great-aunt with them. He wondered if the dragon would agree to the idea if he bought her a hat, too? He might have to explain his reasons to Lady Hermione in private if she was not to reject the plan out of hand.

He didn't have a carriage, either, at Ermcombe, but they might have one at Harford which wouldn't be taken to London. Perhaps they would have a barouche or a landau which wouldn't be suitable for travelling to London. He would have to ask the Harford groom what was in the coach house next time he visited.

Another visit was inevitable, he told himself, after all, he was owed a demonstration by Robbie the dog.

Dark Secret

Peter took care to dress soberly for church the next afternoon. He was aware he had a personal reputation in need of repair, not just for the formidable Lady Hermione, but now for her family, too. He had no doubt she would have blackened his character in the eyes of the Harfords as soon as she knew he was there.

Then he could also see the people at the Ermcombe house and estate probably had a dim view of his careless father, and by extension himself, as a result of years of neglect. It was not just the estate which needed repair, he could see it was his entire family's reputation.

He hadn't met the vicar yet, but who knew? He might be determined to save Peter's soul as well. He hoped not. He had enough to contend with already.

Then, later today, he needed to write a long and detailed letter to his father. Did the marquess fully appreciate how much he was punishing his son? If not,

Peter wanted to be sure he did, although the letter would have to be carefully worded, as antagonising his father would not be good at this point — especially if he wanted his father to send help in the form of somebody who knew how to manage an estate.

In the church there were some pews to the side of the altar and fenced off from the main body of the church. In previous times, someone had decided it would not do for the aristocratic members of the congregation to mix with the unwashed majority.

As Peter headed towards those pews, Baron Harford gave him a friendly nod and Lady Harford beamed at him. So it seemed he was not entirely beyond the pale. Miss Sarah leant towards her sister and whispered something to her. Lady Hermione gave him a frosty glare.

As he sat down, he saw most of the congregation was staring at him in blatant curiosity.

The vicar mounted to the pulpit, arranged some papers, nodded to Peter in a friendly manner and cleared his throat.

'Give me justice, O God, and defend my cause against the wicked; rescue me from deceitful and unjust men,' the vicar said, starting the service.

Peter blinked, before realising the vicar was unlikely to have heard already about Smith and his hurried departure. It did happen to be apt for today, but it was surely coincidence and most likely a standard text for this particular Sunday in the ecclesiastical year. On the other hand, Lady Hermione might think it was a reference to him.

'It's Lord Peter,' her sister had whispered.

If Anne had had ears like Robbie, she would have pricked them up. She heard the little gate to the raised area of pews open and then footsteps sounding hollow on the wooden floor.

There were no greetings in the quiet of the church, but she was almost sure she felt Great-aunt Hermione stiffen as she sat next to Anne. Then there was the slight distant sound of the vicar going up to the pulpit.

Anne always listened to the vicar. He wasn't a great orator, but it was something to do and his sermons were something to think about. But today she wasn't as attentive as normal. Somehow she was very aware of Lord Peter sitting nearby and she wondered what he might think of the vicar and his sermon.

Then she wondered about the coming week. Her parents and Sarah were going to London tomorrow, leaving her with Great-aunt Hermione. Lord Peter had said he would come to see what Robbie could do, but would Anne's disapproving chaperone even allow him into the house?

Later that afternoon, Peter made his preparations for the following day, which was March 25, Lady Day, the quarter day. In normal circumstances, it would not be him paying wages to the servants and collecting rents from the tenants, but these were not normal circumstances.

Harford and Davis had given him a

brief run-down of how these things were done and what records to make. It didn't sound difficult, but so far at Ermcombe it was the unexpected which had been catching him out.

On the positive side, he had calculated the rents received would more than cover the wages he expected to pay. He assumed all the tenants would actually pay, considering he had told them he was cutting their rents by half. At least he still had his quarterly allowance, mostly unspent, which he could use to cover any more unpleasant surprises.

★ ★ ★

Anne stood at the front door with Great-aunt Hermione as they waved goodbye to her parents and Sarah.

'You can stop waving now, dear, they're out of sight,' Hermione said.

Anne dropped her hand and sighed. She felt neglected, abandoned, jealous. She would have liked to go to London, too. She understood why she had been left behind, but it still hurt.

'We must think of things to do while they are away,' Hermione said, patting Anne on the shoulder.

'I think I shall take a walk around the garden,' Anne said, not wanting to talk about it. She might have a little weep in a quiet corner and hope nobody could see her.

'Don't catch a chill by being out too long. It's very cool this morning,' Hermione said.

A cold nose had pushed into Anne's hand at the mention of a walk. She stroked his head and grasped the leather handle fitted to Robbie's shoulders before setting off around the outside of the house. At least Robbie wouldn't desert her.

★ ★ ★

Peter sat at the steward's big desk which had been swept clean of clutter. He had found a fresh ledger, not wanting to use the old ones. The tenants came in first, paid their rent and Peter made a note.

One or two of the farmers expressed their gratitude, again, that Smith's fraud had been discovered.

Then he paid each of the servants. All in all, Peter didn't find the process particularly hard, and the general good humour amongst everyone was gratifying.

At the end, he saw Richards was hovering nearby, clearly wanting to speak to him.

'What is it, Richards?'

'Well, sir, the servants asked me to thank you for uncovering the way Smith had been robbing us all. Then we were wondering if you intended continuing Smith's arrangement about the cellars.'

'Arrangement? Cellars?'

Peter didn't like the sound of this. Not another bad surprise? Anything arranged by Smith was going to be dubious at best and criminal at worst.

'Yes, sir. Perhaps I should show you?'

Peter rose from the desk with a feeling of dread in his stomach. He had not thought of any need to inspect the house since his arrival and had a suspicion it was going to be another of his oversights.

'By all means, lead the way.'

The butler led the way down to the cellars and opened the door. He swung it wide, holding aloft a lantern. The light shone on two rows of barrels and several boxes.

'What is this?' Peter asked, although he thought he already knew.

'Mostly brandy, my lord, with some lace and other items, too.'

'Is this contraband?'

'Yes, sir. After bringing it ashore, the free-traders store it here for a few days before distributing it inland. They bring it up river to the nearby jetty and then on to the house. Smith used to give the servants a guinea each to keep quiet. Some of the local farmers' men would lend a hand and Smith would keep a barrel back as payment too.'

Peter was dismayed. It explained the unexpected quality of the brandy he had been drinking in the evening, but this was yet another complication he didn't need.

Presumably nobody had mentioned it before, as Smith paid them not to and Peter had been an unknown quantity. It was only revealed now, as they could see Smith had been robbing them, but Peter was clearly on their side.

However, the last thing Peter needed at the moment was to be associated with smugglers, if he was to mend his, and his family's, reputations. He would have to tell his father, as his father should know the full extent of what had been going on.

His father was a member of a government opposed to smuggling, so it was quite impossible to allow this to continue. Making a fuss to the authorities would be publicity neither he nor his father would want. It would be best to end it quietly and move on as if nothing had happened.

'Richards, I can't have this going on. I don't know who is involved and I don't wish to know. Please send word, however you can, this is not to continue. The goods which are here are to be removed as soon as convenient and without my knowledge. Then there will be no more.'

'Very good, sir. There is an outside door to the cellar so you will not be disturbed when it is removed.'

'Once it is all gone, ensure the outside door is locked. Ask Mrs Needham to come and find me, if you would. It's time I inspected the rest of the house.'

Peter's tour of the house revealed almost everything was shrouded in Holland covers. So far, the only rooms he had used were his bedroom, the breakfast room, study and steward's office. If he were to have any visitors, at least the public rooms needed to be cleaned and aired.

He should expect visits from the vicar and probably others. Being reclusive was no good and would cause more talk he didn't need. No, he should expect and welcome a few visitors. Everything needed to look normal and respectable. Now there was a little money to hand for making modest improvements, it was time to start cleaning the house and gardens. It would take a while, but he had to start somewhere.

'Mrs Needham, the reception and drawing-rooms need opened up. I am supposing you will need some help, so make enquiries and hire another housemaid. We can add more maids later on when we can afford them.'

'Thank you, sir, I shall get on with it straight away. It will be nice to be opening up the house again.'

Peter thought he ought to hire another gardener and a gatekeeper, too, but this could wait a day or two until he had time to go into Plymouth. Perhaps a second groom and second footman as well. It crossed his mind the men he hired could be out of work again at the end of the quarter, if his father sold the estate, but he dismissed the idea.

Now he had gained a purpose in life, and he was determined to put everything to rights, even if he had to do it slowly. At the same time, he would show his father he had worth and should have been given something useful to do years ago.

He wasn't going to say anything explicit, but perhaps his father would recognise the evils of neglecting an unimportant estate and neglecting an unimportant son, too.

Music to His Ears

Peter was in a positive mood. He felt as if he was getting a grip on things. He should do work of some kind this morning, but the Harfords should be well on the way to London, so perhaps he would call on Lady Hermione and Miss Harford. The ladies would probably appreciate the extra company now they were on their own.

He could also tell Davis how everything had gone on Monday. A brisk ride would do him good and it was a convenient destination, wasn't it?

He realised he was trying to justify the visit to himself. However, he was master here and he didn't need to explain himself to anyone.

'Richards, have my horse brought around in half an hour. I shall be visiting Harford House.'

★   ★   ★

As he trotted along, he remembered last time he had called, other than for dinner. He was still owed a demonstration of Robbie the dog's abilities. However, it might never happen if Lady Hermione denied him entry to the house. He would soon find out.

Gerrard, the butler, greeted him affably enough and took his card upstairs. He returned shortly.

'Lady Hermione will see you, my lord.'

As Peter followed Gerrard upstairs to the morning-room, he could hear a piano being played somewhere in the house. A piece would be played, then there was a pause and the same piece would be played again.

'Good morning, Lord Peter,' Lady Hermione said, giving him a perfunctory nod.

'Good morning, Lady Hermione, I hope I find you well?'

'Well enough, thank you. To what do we owe your call this morning?'

'Owe? Well, nothing really, it is merely a social call. However, if you should see

Davis would you give him my thanks, if you please, and tell him everything went well at the Quarter Day.'

She studied him thoughtfully for a moment. Perhaps, he thought, she wondered why he had called upon her and not upon Davis.

'Were you hoping to see my great-niece?'

Blunt speaking, he thought, but then, he expected nothing else.

'She had volunteered to give me a demonstration of her dog's abilities, but I gather she is practising the piano.'

'Yes, she has a lesson from her piano teacher this morning and cannot be disturbed. Tell me, my lord, are you really so interested in her dog or do you have designs upon Anne instead? You may think it would be easy to take advantage of a blind girl, but I have no intention of letting it happen.'

'Good heavens! I assure you, my lady, my behaviour is entirely honourable and I would never take advantage of an innocent, whether she was blind or not.

'No, it is simply that I felt compassion for her. The first time we met, I felt she was a bit ignored. I even wondered if she was simple-minded, not realising she was blind.

'The second time, I discovered she was far from that and she has a very engaging personality. I also saw she was hurt and disappointed not to be taken to the milliner's in Plymouth with her sister. Surely any young girl would like a new bonnet, even if she can't see it? As a third son, I know what it is to be overlooked.'

Peter stopped talking. He realised he had said more than he had intended. Had he been provoked by Lady Hermione's blunt speaking? She was looking at him in a very considering way.

'I did not know about the milliner, it was before I arrived, and I expect you are correct. I would certainly have taken her to the shop,' she said with a frown.

He suspected she was very fond of her great-niece perhaps more than she was concerned about his disreputable past.

He wanted to find out, because he liked her great-niece, too.

'I would have liked to take her to the milliner's myself to alleviate her disappointment. However, this would, of course, have been most improper and entirely out of the question. On the other hand, perhaps I could take you to the milliner's and buy you a new bonnet?

'I'm sure you realise living in Devon requires the purchase of a suitable hat. It would be a gift from me to welcome you to the county.

'Naturally, we need not mention who is actually paying for it, since it would not be very proper for me to be buying a new hat for a respectable widowed lady, either. We would not want to cause unwelcome gossip and scandal. Especially in view of my reputation, even if it is not well known in these parts. Then if your great-niece is with you and you happen to notice a hat she might like, one could be bought for her, too.'

Peter carefully maintained a straight face. He knew he might be called impertinent and thrown out. He studied Lady Hermione to try to gauge her reaction. He suspected she was trying not to smile.

'You are a glib rogue, Lord Peter. You could probably charm the birds down from the trees if you wished. I should probably have you thrown out. Would Friday be convenient?'

He couldn't help grinning.

'Shall we say about eleven o'clock? I only have a curricle at my disposal, but I believe there is a landau in the coach house here which would be more suitable.'

'Quite so. We shall see you on Friday, my lord.'

Lady Hermione unbent enough to offer her hand which Peter bowed over.

Peter made his way back down the stairs slowly so he could listen to Miss Harford's lesson on the piano as he went. As he stood at the front door, putting on his coat and hat, Peter felt very pleased.

He hoped he had made another small step in redeeming himself. Who knew if word might be passed back to his grand-mother and thence to his father? Every little would help his cause.

There was now slightly less than a quarter left on the calendar before his personal judgement day and there was no time to waste. He hoped this foray into the Plymouth millinery trade would not be time wasted.

★   ★   ★

Once Anne had finished her piano lesson, she and Robbie went to join Lady Hermione. A housemaid arrived moments later with a tea tray.

'I do wonder sometimes, Anne,' Hermione said, 'why you play a piece over and over again when to my ear you had it perfectly the first time.'

'Mostly it is to help me memorise it, but now and again my teacher wants me to change the emphasis I am giving it.'

'Your tea is on the table in front of you, dear,' Lady Hermione said. 'While you were having your lesson, Lord Peter called.'

'Lord Peter?' Anne said, freezing for a moment as she reached for her tea-cup. Her heart fluttered for an instant, then she realised he hadn't lingered to see her. She would have liked to speak with him again, she thought, as she took the biscuit from her saucer and gave it to Robbie. Robbie crunched the biscuit noisily.

'Yes, he has invited us to go with him into Plymouth on Friday. He thought we might like his escort to visit the milliner.'

Anne was puzzled. Why would he take them to a milliner?

'Has he noticed there is something amiss with our hats? Did he notice a defect in them when we all went to church? How humiliating if he feels he needs to take us to the milliner to have it rectified.'

'No, no, this is not it at all. It's because he noticed you were very sad to be left behind when your mother took Sarah to the milliner's for new hats. He said it was because he was a third son who had sometimes been overlooked, and thus had fellow feeling for you when you were overlooked as well.'

Anne's eyes widened in surprise. He had noticed? He hadn't said anything except about her not going to London. He had remembered as well and now he was trying to make her feel better?

'It is . . . It is very kind of him to do this,' Anne said.

'It might be kind or, if I were to be cynical, I might think he had an ulterior motive.'

'What do you mean by an ulterior motive?'

'I mean the man is apparently a rake with a disgraceful reputation who has been sent down here by his father to stop him embarrassing his family. Perhaps he is bored and intends to amuse himself by ruining an innocent blind girl while he is here.'

'Oh!'

Anne wasn't entirely clear what was involved in ruination nor what Lord Peter might have been doing in London.

Somehow she didn't feel she could ask her great-aunt Hermione for more details. Regardless, it seemed the summer might not be quite as flat and boring as she had expected.

'When Lord Peter is with you, you are to be accompanied by myself or Mabel without fail. *Without fail.* There is to be no wandering off alone with him, whatever he might say. I shall instruct Mabel, too, in her duty as chaperone when I am not with you. Is this clearly understood?'

'Yes, Great-aunt Hermione.'

'Good. You might also call me simply 'Aunt'. 'Great-aunt' is more ageing than I find necessary. Of course, it could be he really is a kind man, despite his reputation. Actions speak louder than words, so we will see.'

Anne thought Hermione was kind, too, despite appearing at first to be ferocious. When Anne had been younger, she and Sarah had been rather frightened of her. Now Anne was older, she could see Hermione was very confident and had strong opinions, but she was sure there was a warm heart hidden in there some-where.

'Also,' Hermione continued, 'there is no need to mention to anybody it will be Lord Peter paying for our bonnets. Strictly speaking, it is improper for him to buy either of us a hat and we do not wish to start any scandalous rumours, do we? However, I think he might be hurt if we didn't allow him to do so. So we will be discreet.'

Goodness, Anne thought. Aunt Her-mione was going to allow him to buy them hats, even when she said it was a bit scandalous for him to do so? And it was be done secretly? Whatever next? Perhaps her aunt was not quite so prim and proper as Anne had always believed.

Anne would have to be careful how much her mother heard about this, in case she was shocked. It was looking as if hav-ing Hermione for a chaperone might be more entertaining than Anne had antic-ipated even if, at the same time, she was going to be strict. Anne's next letter to Sarah would have to be worded carefully.

A Handsome Escort

Friday turned out to be cloudy and grey, with an unseasonable chill and a sharp breeze. Peter was glad of his thick overcoat as he rode over to Harford House. He thought they would have done better with a closed carriage and hot bricks, but a landau was all they had. The travelling carriage was in London by now. At least with a landau they could lift the roof to give a little protection from the weather.

When he arrived, the carriage was standing at the front of the house. He was pleased to see this one had glass windows to the doors, although the carriage would still be inevitably draughty. A groom took his horse away and the front door opened as he mounted the steps. The ladies were waiting for him in the hall. He was relieved to see they were prompt and warmly dressed.

'Good morning, ladies,' he said, executing a bow. Anne curtseyed and Lady Hermione gave him a slight bow in return.

'It is chilly today,' he said, 'but I understand it is little more than an hour into Plymouth, so we should not get too cold. Provided, that is, we don't meet a farm cart in one of these narrow lanes.'

'We must hope not,' Lady Hermione said. 'Anne, do take Lord Peter's arm and let him assist you into the carriage.'

Hermione raised an eyebrow at Peter, waiting to see if he would take the hint and act appropriately. He stepped forward and took Anne's half-raised hand, setting it on his sleeve. He covered her gloved hand with his.

'A few steps to the door,' he said, leading her forward but pausing at the top of the steps.

'And three steps down,' she said with a smile, suiting her actions to her words.

He led her forward a few steps more before pausing again.

'The step of the landau is directly in front of you. Do you need more help or can you manage from here?'

She felt for the step with her foot and

then grasped the handle beside the door. A footman hovered to the side in case he was needed, but Anne released Peter's arm and stepped confidently up into the carriage. It appeared she was familiar with the vehicle.

Peter then stepped to the side and offered a hand to assist Lady Hermione. She nodded silent approval at him before joining Anne. Peter climbed up to the rear facing seat, took blankets which were resting there and passed them to Lady Hermione. She spread them on both ladies' laps as the footman closed the door.

Peter glanced at the ladies as their carriage rumbled away down the gravel drive. Lady Hermione looked impassive. Anne looked pleased, and so, for a reason he didn't stop to identify, Peter felt pleased, too.

'I am supposing the coachman knows where to go?' Peter asked.

'I understand the Mayflower Inn is a respectable establishment and then there is a short walk to Madame Violette, the milliner,' Lady Hermione said. 'Gerrard said Madame Violette is the shop patronised by Lady Harford.'

'I am further supposing we shall take a light luncheon when we arrive?'

'Yes, indeed. I also gather from Gerrard, the Mayflower can provide a suitable meal.'

They lapsed into silence as Peter mulled it over. He fully expected there to be a private parlour available, but what could the Mayflower provide to eat which wouldn't cause Anne any awkwardness or embarrassment? He would have to make a discreet enquiry of the landlord on arrival.

Anne felt bubbly with excitement, even if it was just a shopping trip. Previously a trip to the milliner meant a bonnet was bought for her and she was barely consulted in the choice. This time, Aunt Hermione had assured her, the choice was to be entirely Anne's. And they were being escorted by the son of a marquess whom she had also been assured was very handsome. She liked him. If he was a bit rakish, then it made him more exciting, and she had her aunt with her to keep her safe. Safe from what, she wasn't sure, but never mind.

When she got home, she must get Mabel to write a letter to Sarah who would go green with envy. She felt a little guilty at her wicked intention, then she brushed it aside. It was about time she had her turn to be indulged.

She worried a little about luncheon. How would she cope without guidance from Gerrard or her mother? She felt Hermione take her hand and squeeze it gently. Anne imagined she might have been frowning without realising it. She turned her head towards Hermione and smiled, giving Hermione's hand a little squeeze in return.

* * *

At the Mayflower Inn, the landlord escorted them all to a private parlour.

'Tea?' Peter asked the ladies, who both nodded.

'Tea for three, please,' Peter said, and indicated the landlord should precede him from the room before following him out.

He came back a few minutes later, having discussed what was available for lunch.

'Ladies, I have asked for a light lunch of sausage rolls, a ham and chicken pie, and some Cornish pasties followed by Banbury cakes and fruit.

'I am not familiar with Cornish pasties but I am assured they are a local delicacy, although perhaps a little rustic. If they do not suit, we can send them back. Have you tried them before?'

'Not I,' Lady Hermione said. 'What are they like?'

'Oh, I have,' Anne said, 'we had some once for a picnic. They are meat and potato encased in pastry. We ate them with our hands. Aunt Hermione, do you think it would be improper to eat them this way indoors?'

Lady Hermione gave Peter an understanding nod with wide eyes and raised eyebrows. He smiled quietly in return.

'No, dear, we are quite private here and I'm sure a sort of indoor picnic would be quite in order. Besides, it is far too chilly to be picnicking outside today.'

The tea and food arrived within a few minutes. While Lady Hermione occupied herself pouring the tea, Peter served Anne with food.

'Miss Harford,' he said, 'I have put a sausage roll at nine o'clock and a slice of the pie at twelve o'clock. At three o'clock there is a Cornish pasty with one end wrapped in a serviette. There is a cup of tea on the right hand side, just beyond your plate.

'If you give me your right hand I have a serviette for you to put on your lap. Is there anything else you would like at the moment?'

He spoke quietly as if there would have been other people to overhear him other than Lady Hermione.

Anne put her hand forward and Peter placed the serviette into it. Before she took it, she squeezed Peter's hand gently.

'Thank you, my lord,' she said just as quietly. 'You are very kind and thoughtful.'

She took the serviette, opened it out and placed it on her lap.

Peter watched carefully to make sure all was well. As he looked up to see to his own food, he noticed Lady Hermione had been watching his interaction with Anne. She glanced at him briefly with a glimmer of a smile before attending to her own plate.

Once they had eaten and drunk their fill, they headed off down the street to the milliner, Anne holding her aunt's arm. As they entered the shop, a smart but modestly dressed lady of middle years hurried forward to greet them. This was presumably Madame Violette.

'Good afternoon, milady,' she said with a curtsey. 'How may I help you?'

'Good afternoon. I am Lady Danvers, this is Lord Wilson, and this is Miss Harford. I understand you have made hats for Lady Harford?'

'Yes indeed, milady. Lady Harford is a

most valued customer.'

'Good. I and my great-niece both require new bonnets. Perhaps you could show us what you have available now.'

Peter was glad Lady Hermione had taken charge. He was unfamiliar with milliners, not having sisters and never having kept a mistress. His mother certainly didn't require assistance in choosing a hat, so he was vaguely uneasy in this foreign environment.

He hoped he wouldn't be called upon to say if something was fashionable or not. He could express an opinion on whether or not he liked a hat, but that was about all.

'Perhaps the ladies would sit at this table, and his lordship over here,' Madame Violette said, pointing out some chairs, 'then I will fetch some examples for you to consider.'

A selection of hats were placed on the table and then replaced with others as Lady Hermione expressed her likes and dislikes. Madame Violette looked slightly puzzled that each one was described to

Anne who then felt it with her hands, so Anne's blindness was explained. Finally Hermione settled on a light brown bonnet with a dark brown velvet interior and a brown fur trim around the brim.

'What do you think of this one, Lord Peter?' Lady Hermione asked.

Peter's attention suddenly focused on the bonnet on her head. He had been wool-gathering about what more he needed to do at home and when he might hear from his father. She turned her head a little each way.

'Oh, it looks very nice,' he said, frowning a little, 'but did you not want something more summery?'

'No, I brought summer hats with me, but frankly I am finding this cold weather uncomfortable. I thought something a little warmer would be better.'

'In that case I think it is an excellent choice,' Peter said. He certainly wasn't going to get involved in a more complex discussion and agreement seemed wise.

'Good. Now let us find something for Anne.'

The process was repeated but with hats more suitable for a young lady. Peter's thoughts drifted again, until his opinion was suddenly sought once more. This time Anne was wearing a blue poke bonnet trimmed with lace around the brim.

'Lord Peter,' Anne said, 'what do you think of this one?'

'Turn your head a little each way,' her great-aunt said, 'so he can see it properly.'

Peter thought the blue matched her eyes perfectly, but considering she was blind, he wasn't sure this was tactful, or if it was something he could say. It was certainly a very fetching hat on the head of a very fetching young lady.

'I . . . I . . . er . . .' he stammered. Now he wasn't sure what he could say without sounding flirtatious, which would surely result in a reprimand from the young lady's fierce chaperone. To his surprise, Lady Hermione chuckled.

'I do believe Lord Peter has been rendered speechless,' she said.

'I think it is a very pretty hat,' he managed, rather feebly, at last.

'Really? Are you quite sure? I will have to take your word for it you know, so you must answer entirely truthfully,' Anne said uncertainly.

'Yes. Yes, I am quite sure,' Peter said, realising more enthusiasm was required. 'If you were walking down Piccadilly wearing this hat, you would turn all the men's heads.'

Anne gave him a broad smile and then her smile suddenly faded to be replaced by sadness.

'But I would never know, would I, if I couldn't see them?'

Peter mentally kicked himself for choosing a poor example.

'Yes, Miss Harford, but if you were walking down Piccadilly with your hand on my arm, I would be sure to tell you how it was. Not only that, but I would be taking great pleasure in walking with such a pretty young lady on my arm. It is an excellent choice of bonnet.'

He rather suspected he would be glaring or growling at the other men, too, but he wasn't going to mention that. On the other hand, he really could imagine them walking down Piccadilly together, but he couldn't say this, either. Definitely not with Lady Hermione sitting there looking back at him thoughtfully. Had he spoken too extravagantly? However, she didn't say anything and Anne was smiling broadly again, so he thought it best if he said no more.

'My ladies, shall I put your new bonnets into hat boxes for his lordship to carry?' Madame Violette asked.

'Certainly not,' Peter said. 'You may put their old hats into boxes for me to carry. I wish to see them wearing the new ones.'

As Madame Violette handed him the boxes, he gave her his card.

'You may send the bill to me at Ermcombe,' he said quietly.

Madame Violette's eyes flicked briefly from him to Anne and back before she smiled at him.

Peter could see what she was thinking, but he didn't really care. If she started a rumour it would do him no harm and might do Miss Harford some good if people starting paying her more attention.

* * *

'Ladies,' Peter said, as the carriage carried them home, 'I hope you will agree the expedition has been successful. It certainly looks it from where I am sitting.'

'It has been good to get out of the house for a while,' Lady Hermione said. 'Wouldn't you agree, Anne?'

'Oh, yes, Aunt, it has been most agreeable,' Anne said with a broad smile. 'We must thank Lord Peter for escorting us.'

'It was my pleasure,' he said. 'Now I am looking forward to a demonstration of Robbie's abilities.'

'Aunt Hermione, when do you think it would be a good time for his lordship to call?'

'Perhaps Lord Peter would like to join us for a light lunch tomorrow?'

'I shall look forward to it,' he said.

A Chance to Dance?

Lunch over, they repaired to the drawing-room. Anne stood at one end holding on to Robbie, who sat beside her.

'Aunt Hermione, I am going to walk down the room. Would you put some obstructions in my way, please?'

Lady Hermione placed a small table and a chair in the middle of the floor.

'Lord Peter, the servants normally have instructions not to move furniture around, so I know where things are, for the times Robbie is not with me. In this case you will note I have little idea where my aunt has placed the obstructions.'

Anne really hoped Robbie would do as he normally did. It would be embarrassing to arrange this little demonstration and then have something go wrong.

On one hand, it wouldn't matter if it went a bit awry, she was unlikely to hurt herself. On the other hand, she wanted to impress his lordship. He had been kind and attentive so far and she didn't want to lose his regard by appearing silly.

'Ready, Anne,' Lady Hermione said.

'Come, Robbie,' Anne said, walking down the room.

Just as they reached the chair, Robbie stopped and Anne stopped, too.

'Show me the way, Robbie,' she said.

The dog moved to the side and led Anne past the chair.

'Oh, bravo!' Peter exclaimed.

Anne smiled. It felt as if the praise was for both her and Robbie.

Robbie stopped again as they reached the table.

'Good dog, Robbie,' Anne said, 'to the sofa.'

Robbie went around Anne and she turned with him before he led her to the sofa, where he stopped again. Anne felt for the edge of the sofa and then sat down.

'Good dog, well done, Robbie, you're such a good boy,' she said, stroking his head.

Robbie's ears went limp and he wagged his tail across the carpet. Peter went to replace the chair and table, but Lady Hermione waved him away.

'Thank you, Lord Peter, but I made a note of their original positions, so let me replace them exactly where they were.'

'Lord Peter,' Anne said, 'would you take my reticule, please, and put it somewhere in the room. Not too close and somewhere on the floor but not in plain sight. While you are doing this, I shall cover Robbie's eyes and ears so he can't see or hear where you have put it.'

She held out her reticule until she felt him take it from her, before placing her hands on Robbie's head. She felt Aunt Hermione take the seat next to her.

'When you have done it, my lord, please come and join us on the sofa,' Anne said.

'Move a little closer to me, my dear,' her aunt said, 'to make room for his lordship.'

Anne was a little surprised at the way her aunt was obviously intending Lord Peter to sit next to Anne, rather than with a chaperone between the two of them. Was her aunt mellowing towards Lord Peter?

Anne felt a little frisson of anticipation of him being close to her. She felt the cushion depress as he sat down and could smell his fresh lemony cologne which had a hint of something spicy, too. Now she realised she recognised it from one of their previous meetings, although it had been faint then and she had paid little attention at the time. She removed her hands from Robbie.

'Oh, Robbie! Where is my reticule? Robbie, smell, smell! Find my reticule, Robbie!'

The dog stood and looked about, before slowly going around the room, inspecting all the furniture.

Now and again he would lift his nose and Peter could see the dog appeared to be smelling the cushions. Peter had placed the reticule on the floor behind a fire-screen.

As the dog approached the fireplace he stopped, and sniffed the air before then going straight towards the fire-screen. A quick inspection and the dog appeared from behind the screen with the bag in his mouth. He trotted over to Anne and she felt him nudge her knee with the reticule. She reached down and took it from him.

'Good dog, Robbie, well done,' Anne said, stroking his head.

'This is truly remarkable,' Peter said. 'I have never seen anything like it. Is there anything else he can do?'

'Many things, my lord. Robbie, right paw,' Anne said, holding out her hand.

The dog put his right paw into her hand.

'However, this is little more than a party trick. Robbie, left paw,' she said, holding out her hand again.

Robbie put his left paw into her hand.

'But more usefully, he knows the words for many objects such as 'handkerchief' or 'slippers', for example. It can be a god-send when I have mislaid something and he can find it for me. If it was just me, I could be searching for hours without success. Of course, I know I could call a servant, but it's more interesting this way and besides, I think Robbie is likely to be quicker in many cases. I think he enjoys having something useful to do.'

'It is quite astonishing. I think if I were to tell some of my friends about Robbie, they would not believe me.'

Anne felt a moment of alarm. Did this mean he was going away? She was enjoying his company and would be disappointed if he were to leave Devon after having arrived so recently.

'Will you be going back to London soon then, my lord?'

'No, not for some time yet. I expect to be here all summer, at least.'

'Do you not miss your friends?'

There was a pause and she heard him sigh.

'To be frank, Miss Harford, not as much as I had expected. I can see much of what we used to do were simply idle pursuits because we had nothing better to do. I haven't been long here in Devon, but I am already finding it much more worthwhile down here.'

'You don't miss the parties and the balls? I'm sure you must have attended many.'

'Yes, I have, but there comes a point where it seems repetitive and almost tedious. However, speaking of balls, do you attend any in Plymouth?'

It was Anne's turn to sigh. She would love to dance, but she knew it was impossible. She would have liked to play piano for an audience, but it simply wasn't done either by someone like her in society. Her father would never permit it, and they had few visitors.

'No, my lord, I cannot dance if I cannot see where I am going and whilst I could listen to the music, it is less than inspiring. I have been once or twice, but I always feel the other ladies were probably pitying me, so it is an uncomfortable business.'

'You could always waltz,' Peter said.

'Waltz?' both ladies said together, one surprised, the other shocked.

'Yes, you don't need to see where you are going in the waltz, provided your partner is able to do so.'

'My lord,' Lady Hermione said, 'I don't know where you may have waltzed, but in many places, including this one, it is considered the height of impropriety.'

'Really? It has been danced at Almack's for the last two or three years, so I do believe it must now be accepted as respectable.'

'Almack's? Are you quite sure?' Hermione asked.

'Yes, quite sure, I have waltzed there myself,' Peter replied.

Anne thought this was interesting, but it didn't seem very relevant. She didn't know how to waltz, she wouldn't be allowed to waltz, and besides, where would the opportunity arise in this part of the country?

'I'm afraid it is academic, my lord, since I don't know how to waltz, and there will be no suitable occasion anyway,' Anne said.

'Once you know how, then will be the time to consider when there might be an occasion. In the meantime I can teach you.'

'Teach me? But how is this possible?'

'It is easily possible, because for the waltz we don't require other dancers to make up a set, we just need someone to play the music. I can be your partner and show you how it's done.'

There was a pause in the conversation. Anne wondered if Lord Peter was looking at her aunt to see if she would play for them. She had no idea if Hermione could play the piano nor if she would allow him to teach her anyway. She heard her take a deep breath and let it out slowly.

'Don't ask me,' Lady Hermione said, 'my piano playing is poor, my hands are too stiff, I don't know any waltz tunes and I very much doubt we have any waltz sheet music in the house.'

'No, we don't,' Anne said, 'and I couldn't play either if I were to be dancing at the same time.'

'I would wager your music teacher can play a waltz tune,' Peter said.

'Hmm,' Hermione said quietly, then

more loudly, 'very well. We shall ask Mr Healey next week. Lord Peter, be so good as to present yourself at eleven o'clock on Wednesday and we shall see what can be done.'

Anne felt the sofa cushions move as he stood up. Her aunt had clearly hinted it was time for him to go.

'Certainly. I shall look forward to it. Good afternoon, ladies.'

Anne was elated. She had been expecting a boring summer, but now she was going to learn to waltz and with a man she was coming to like rather a lot. He must like her too, if he was being so kind and considerate. She was also amazed Aunt Hermione was permitting it.

She hadn't expected to be glad she wasn't in London with the others, but now she found she was pleased to be at home. Anne wondered if Sarah was waltzing at balls in London. Had she been given permission by the patronesses of Almack's? Was she even going to Almack's?

Would the letter of introduction to the

marquess have made it possible? Even if it had, would her parents allow Sarah to waltz? So many questions. She would have to send a letter to Sarah. But did she dare mention she was having waltzing lessons? Perhaps not — she wouldn't want her father to write back forbidding it. Still, she could ask her sister if she had been to Almack's and, if so, was she allowed to waltz there?

In any case, she knew Sarah would need lessons before she waltzed, because she hadn't learned while she was here at home.

Her sister would be very aggravated if she wasn't allowed to do the new dance and then returned at the end of the season to find Anne already knew how. It would make a change for her to be able to do something which Sarah couldn't.

* * *

On his way home, Peter was feeling lighthearted. When he had thought back about the entertainments in London, which he was not now attending, he realised he wasn't missing them at all. He could see they were all rather similar and a bit repetitive.

This explained why he and his friends had been behaving outrageously the way they had. It had been to inject some variety in their lives.

Moving to Devon had turned out to be a very refreshing change. He was looking forward to teaching Miss Harford to waltz much more than he had looked forward to dancing with some of those insipid débutantes in Mayfair. Those débutantes had thought it clever, or fashionable, to look bored. Anne had looked as if she was delighted at the prospect of learning to waltz.

Peter was feeling rather fond of her and he felt happy to know she was so pleased at the idea. When he had looked up, it was to find Lady Hermione gazing at him thoughtfully. He supposed she had relented for Anne's benefit, but no doubt was going to be watching him

115

closely to be sure he behaved. She need not worry; he would never hurt Anne.

Cautious Steps

On Wednesday, Peter presented himself at Harford House a quarter of an hour before 11 o'clock. He was very conscious of Lady Hermione's critical eyes and wanted to be sure he was there on time, but not so early to cause any awkwardness.

'Good morning, my lord,' a smiling Gerrard said as he opened the door to him.

'Good morning,' Peter said, handing over his hat, gloves, riding crop and a cloth bag. 'Has the music teacher arrived?'

'Yes, sir,' Gerrard said, helping him off with his coat. 'Mr Healey has already gone up to the music room.'

'Good. Now I need to change from my riding boots to my shoes.' He pointed to the cloth bag.

'Ah, I see,' the butler said, nodding his understanding of the purpose of the bag. 'Would you take a seat, my lord, and Joseph will assist you to remove your boots.'

A footman, presumably Joseph, hurried back from the hall closet where he had been hanging up Peter's overcoat. He knelt in front of Peter and grasped the heel of a boot, easing it off before doing the same with the other one. Gerrard passed the shoe bag to Joseph who put Peter's shoes on his feet. The footman took the boots and the empty bag off to the closet.

'May I escort you to the music room, my lord?' Gerrard asked.

Peter followed him upstairs and, as he entered the room, there was a cheerful tune being played on the piano by Anne. Lady Hermione sat nearby and there was a man standing to one side and slightly behind Anne.

'Good morning, Lord Peter,' Lady Hermione said, fairly loudly.

Anne abruptly stopped playing and looked over the piano, approximately towards the door, with a broad smile on her face. Peter bowed to Lady Hermione and then to Anne. He knew she couldn't see him, but he also knew (as did Lady Hermione) that it was the proper thing to do anyway.

'Good morning, ladies.'

'May I present Mr George Healey, the music teacher,' Lady Hermione said.

Peter nodded to him and got a bow in return. Peter was unaccountably pleased to note the music teacher was a slightly portly man, of about the same age as Anne's father.

Anne stood and made her way around the piano, guiding herself with a hand lightly touching the instrument.

'My lord, thank you for coming but I'm afraid there is a slight problem. You see, because I have never danced, I do not have dancing slippers.'

'I have a confession, too,' Peter said, 'I didn't anticipate dancing in Devonshire and so I didn't bring any with me. Thus I stand before you wearing ordinary shoes.

'However, for the purpose of learning the basic steps today, I don't think this will matter. Perhaps if we are to try another lesson next week, we could both visit a shoemaker in Plymouth in the meantime.'

He glanced at Lady Hermione. She raised her eyebrows but made no comment.

'Next week?' Anne asked in surprise.

'Why, yes. I am hoping you will be an adept pupil, but we should not assume instant competence. Shall we begin at once?'

Anne nodded.

'Allow me to take your right hand,' he said.

Anne held out her hand, Peter took it and drew her further into the room and away from the piano. He looked around to be sure they had some space.

'Miss Harford, first I shall show you a basic step without the music. Place your left hand upon my right shoulder.'

Anne lifted her hand tentatively. He took it gently and placed it upon his right shoulder.

'I now place my right hand upon your

waist and then, with my left, lift your right hand to be about the same height as our shoulders. I am standing slightly to your right hand side. This way we do not tread on each other's feet and I can see over your shoulder.

'Thus I am able to see where we are going and guide you around the room without us crashing into the furniture. Or other dancers. There is a gap between us of several inches, so we do not scandalise the patronesses at Almack's.'

'Almack's!' she exclaimed, with a chuckle.

'Not this week, but perhaps some other time.'

He glanced at Lady Hermione, who was shaking her head ruefully. He looked down at Anne who was biting her bottom lip. Yes, he thought, he might like to waltz with her at Almack's some time. However, at the moment, he should concentrate on teaching her the steps.

'Miss Harford, you will feel me move forward with my left foot so you should step back with your right. Like so. Now I will step to my right and you will follow by stepping to your left.'

She hesitated a moment before stepping to the left. Peter supposed she had not been expecting this.

'Now you close your right foot to be beside your left foot. Excellent! These are the fundamental three steps to the waltz. Now we will do the same again except in a mirror image. That is to say as you feel me step back on my right, you will go forward with your left, then step to the right and close your feet.

'Let us do so now . . . and very good, we are now back where we started. We will do all of it again twice more, but as we close our feet we will rise a little on to our toes. Ready?'

She nodded and he led her through the steps again, marking two small square shapes on the floor as they went.

'Very good. Now if Mr Healey would play us a few bars of a waltz, you will hear the rhythm.'

He nodded to Mr Healey who had seated himself at the piano, and Mr

Healey played a short snatch from a waltz.

'Oh, yes,' Anne said, 'I can recognise how it goes.'

'I felt sure you would grasp it straight away as you are an accomplished musician yourself.'

Anne blushed a little at the praise.

'Now let us practise this box step a few times to feel how it works with the music.'

He nodded again to the music teacher who launched into a waltz. Anne immediately went to start but Peter held her for a moment.

'Ah, ah, ah! No, you must wait for your partner to lead you, otherwise we will trip over each other and end in an unseemly and undignified heap on the floor.'

Peter waited for the beat and then led Anne around their little square shape on the floor several times before stopping.

'Thank you, Mr Healey,' he said, and the music teacher stopped playing.

'Miss Harford, I suspect you are going

to be a very quick study as you have picked up the rhythm very well. Now, in a ballroom we would not remain going around and around on our little patch of the floor, but instead we would float down the room, turning as we go. At the corner we would turn and continue across the floor.

'Therefore the next thing you need to learn is a turn. When we are dancing around the room and arrive at a corner, I will be turning you a little bit more so we then face across the room, ready to continue. So now let me show you how to do a natural turn, it's essentially the same as the box step we have been doing, but we rotate as we do it.'

'Is there also an unnatural turn?' Anne asked.

'Yes and no,' Peter said with a smile, 'it is actually called a reverse turn. It's necessary because if we always turn the same way we will end up dizzy and fall over ourselves which would be embarrassing. So we do a few natural turns and then I will lead you into some reverse turns.'

Thirty minutes later, Peter declared it was enough for one day.

'Thank you for the dance, Miss Harford,' he said, with a bow.

'It has been my pleasure,' Anne said as she curtseyed.

'Lord Peter,' Lady Hermione said, 'I think perhaps we will take up your suggestion to go to a cordwainer in Plymouth. Would Friday suit you?'

'Perfectly,' Peter said. 'A similar arrangement as our visit to the milliner?'

'Quite so,' Lady Hermione replied, 'and we thank you for this morning's visit.'

She nodded to him as he bowed to her. He noticed how Anne was grinning at the prospect and he couldn't help but smile broadly, too.

Gerrard appeared at the door, by good butler's magic, to escort him downstairs.

Too Soon for Promises

'Tell me,' Peter said, as Richards poured his morning coffee on Friday morning, 'where is a good bootmaker in Plymouth?'

Richards straightened up, still holding the coffee pot as he considered the question.

'Well, sir, there are three whom I know of which cater to gentlemen. Freeman's, Hardy and Son, and Willis Brothers. However I could not say which one is better than the others. I myself patronise a different establishment which is, er . . . more economical, shall we say, but not really of a standard suitable for a gentleman such as yourself.'

'I see. Do you suppose Mr Gerrard would know which one is to be preferred?'

'More than likely, sir. If not, Mr Davis would undoubtedly know, as he would have paid Lord Harford's account when rendered by the bootmaker.'

'Ah yes, I should have thought of this myself. Thank you, Richards. I shall ask when I call at Harford House this morning.'

Peter arrived at Harford House earlier than arranged, so he would have time to enquire of Davis if Gerrard didn't know. In the event, Gerrard did know and suggested Hardy and Son as the most appropriate, since they made boots for Lord Harford.

He said he thought the others were good, but catered more for naval and army officers, of whom there were so many in Plymouth. He also said Lady Hermione wished to speak to him if he was in good time and so conducted him up to the morning-room.

'Good morning, Lord Peter, I am glad you are a little early as I wanted a word before Anne comes down. Please take a seat.'

Peter bowed and then took the seat indicated. He wondered what Lady Hermione wanted, but she didn't keep him waiting.

'Lord Peter, a casual observer would think you were courting my great-niece, but as you know, I am well aware of your reputation. I will not have Anne hurt and if you are merely amusing yourself it would be better if you did not call again. I do not want Anne imagining something which is not the case.'

Peter took a deep breath whilst he marshalled his thoughts. He was not entirely sure what his intentions were himself. He put his elbows on the arms of the chair and steepled his fingertips against his lips.

'I can understand your concern and must be open with you,' he said, 'on the understanding it stays between us. Lord Harford is already aware of my circumstances. I have no doubt you will be discreet and explain my situation to Anne, as gently as possible, if it should become necessary.'

'You may be confident of my discretion, provided you speak plainly and honestly,' Lady Hermione said.

'Thank you. You will not be surprised

to learn I recently caused my father and my family great embarrassment with my behaviour and that of my friends in London.

'Frankly, I see now how it was a result of idleness, boredom and the lack of any useful purpose. As a result, my father stopped my allowance and sent me down here to see what was wrong with the Ermcombe estate.

'If I can restore the estate to a proper condition by the end of this quarter, it will become mine. If I cannot, it will be sold and I shall be effectively cast off. In the latter case I will find it necessary to seek employment in India, the Americas, the West Indies or elsewhere.'

Peter could see Lady Hermione was a little surprised at his situation, but she made no comment.

'When I made the acquaintance of the Harford family,' he continued, 'I felt sympathy for Miss Anne's situation. I could understand the position she was being put in, and as a sometimes overlooked third son, I knew how it could

129

sometimes be hard to bear.

'I have become unexpectedly fond of Miss Harford, but if it can ever be allowed to come to anything, I really cannot tell.

'I am optimistic of a good outcome for the estate at the end of the quarter, but it is impossible to be sure. If, at that point, I am then making plans to emigrate, I would have nothing to offer anybody and the very last thing I could consider is to take a blind wife with me.

'Even if the estate does become mine, I can make no promises, except to say I would not wish to hurt Miss Harford in any way. Whatever happens, I would hope to remain friends with the Harford family.'

'I see,' Lady Hermione said, 'thank you for being so frank with me. I shall keep the knowledge to myself, but try to dampen any of Anne's expectations in the meantime. I shall hope you will take care not to raise her expectations, either.'

'I shall take care and I shall endeavour not to make my visits too long or too frequent.'

'Very good. Now I think I hear Anne on the stairs talking to her maid, so let us join her and go downstairs.'

'Mabel, I hear the clock chiming eleven!' Anne had said to her maid, who had just that moment finished reading a letter from Sarah.

'Oh, I'm so sorry, miss, I wasn't watching the time,' Mabel said, hurriedly placing the letter on a side table.

'No matter, I only need my boots, pelisse and bonnet. I'm sure they won't go without us.'

'No, miss, but it doesn't do to keep a handsome gentleman waiting,' Mabel said as she knelt to lace up Anne's footwear.

'Do you think he is handsome, then?'

'Coo, yes! I bet Miss Sarah was hoping he would go off to London while she was there. Never mind, now she has an entry to Almack's she'll have plenty of chances to meet gentlemen. Gentlemen with titles, as I'm sure her ladyship is hoping.'

'Yes, Lord Peter's letter must have

done the trick if the marchioness introduced my mother to Lady Cowper. It was kind of Lord Peter to write, otherwise my parents wouldn't have known anybody.'

'There you are, miss,' Mabel said, tying the ribbons of Anne's hat, 'now it's just your gloves.'

Anne felt the bonnet.

'It's the new hat,' Anne said with a smile.

'Yes, miss. You said his lordship had admired it, so it had to be this one. If you take your gloves, I'll go with you downstairs.'

Anne held out a hand and Mabel put the gloves into it, before going to open the bedchamber door.

'Is it cold out?' Anne asked.

'Yes, miss, it was a bit fresh when I took Robbie for a walk, but you'll be fine, you're wearing a warm pelisse.'

As they reached the landing down the first flight of stairs, the morning-room door opened.

'Oh, his lordship was with Lady

Hermione in the morning-room,' Mabel said, and she dropped back behind Anne.

'Miss Harford, good morning,' Peter said, coming out on to the landing. 'May I offer you my arm as we go down to the front door?'

'Good morning, my lord,' Anne said, holding out a hand. 'Thank you.'

Peter took her hand, placed it on his sleeve and covered it with his hand.

'I must say, Miss Harford, you are wearing a vastly fetching hat.'

'Why thank you, sir. A kind gentleman helped me choose it last week.'

'Did he indeed? Well, I am quite jealous of his good fortune that he was able to assist you.'

They both chuckled as they went slowly down the last flight of stairs. Gerrard stood ready with Peter's hat and coat, while Lady Hermione's dresser was waiting there, too, with her hat and a cloak.

★ ★ ★

The outing followed much the same pattern as the previous week except the Banbury cakes were replaced by the landlady's Shrewsbury cakes. After lunch they set off down the street with Anne's hand on her aunt's arm. When they arrived at the shoemaker's shop, they stopped.

'Lord Peter,' Lady Hermione said, 'you may leave us while you go to the bootmaker. We shall await your return here.'

Peter was puzzled for a moment. Lady Hermione lifted a toe and glanced down at it, then looked at Peter with a raised eyebrow. He understood the silent message. He was not going to be permitted any inspection of ladies' ankles.

'Ah, yes, of course,' he said. 'I hope you find something suitable and for my part I will endeavour to return promptly.'

The bootmaker's was only a few shops further down the street. His visit was brief as they had nothing suitable already or part made, so it was simply a question of taking his measurements and a description of what he needed. Since he regarded dancing slippers as functional rather than decorative, this was not complicated.

Once he was back at the shoemaker's, he hesitated outside, not sure what to do. His dilemma was solved by the jangle of the door bell and the emergence of a young shop girl.

'If you please, sir, would you care to step into the front room? Their ladyships are having a fitting in the back room and will not be very long.'

It was a chilly day and Peter was glad to step into the warmth of the shop, even if he had nothing to do. As he sat there, he wondered how his father would respond to the letter Peter had sent.

Hopefully he would be positive and send someone who knew what he was doing. Failing that, Peter would need to scour the employment agencies in Plymouth in hopes of finding a replacement steward.

He supposed his father might simply wash his hands of the whole affair, including him, but he didn't think so. Cutting off his nose to spite his face was not characteristic of his father. If he hadn't wanted a positive outcome for both Peter and the estate, he could have found him a post with the East India Company in Calcutta or Bombay. No, his father would surely send help, even if it was only advice or some cash.

His ruminations were interrupted, and he sprang to his feet, as the ladies emerged from the back room.

'Ah, good, Lord Peter is here,' Lady Hermione said. 'We are ready to go back to the Mayflower, my lord, for tea before returning home.'

'Were you able to get some dancing slippers?' Peter asked, as they walked down the street with Anne on his arm.

'Yes, my lord,' Anne said.

'May I see them?'

'Yes, my lord. Next Wednesday.'

'Oh,' Peter said, 'this, I gather, is to keep me in a fever of anticipation until then.'

'Quite so, sir,' Anne said with a grin.

'Were you able to get some for yourself?'

'No, but I am having some made for me. So I am afraid you must also wait until Wednesday.'

Anne laughed, Peter chuckled and then he saw Lady Hermione had the merest glimmer of a smile on her lips, too. He understood, despite the plain speaking of this morning, Lady Hermione was not averse to some light banter between himself and Anne.

Sinister Warning

'Sir, there is a person here who insists on speaking with you,' Richards said.

'A person? Who insists?'

This was odd, Peter thought. His butler obviously took a dim view of the visitor and yet hadn't been able to turn him away.

'Who is it?'

'You can call me Jory, me lord.' A scruffy individual with a heavily tanned face, pushed past Richards into the study.

'Here, you, I said you were to wait in the hall,' Richards blustered.

'It's about the barrels in your cellar,' Jory said, ignoring the butler.

'You took them away, didn't you?' Peter asked, seeing this Jory must be one of the smugglers.

'Yes, me lord, we did. However, we need to borrer your cellar again next week, so I thought we should come to an arrangement like what we had with your Mr Smith.'

'What? No! Absolutely not,' Peter said. 'I don't want to know what was going on in the past, but there will be no more in the future. I thought I had made it clear.'

'I'm afraid I must insist, me lord. You see, when we bring the boats up the river, the jetty on your land is the only one close to somewhere, like your cellar fr'instance, where we can store the goods for a short time.

'Being as we're so close to Plymouth and His Majesty's Navy, we 'ave to come up the river to be out of sight pretty sharpish and not 'ang about with the unloading neither. So you see, we don't 'ave a lot of choice about 'ow and where it's done.'

'Insist all you want, I want nothing to do with it.'

'It's not a choice,' Jory said, his face darkening, 'it's going to 'appen. Don't you think it won't. I wouldn't want any of yer servants to get 'urt if they try to stop us, would I? Besides, they be wasting their time, there's a lot more of us than 'em.

'And don't you try tipping off the Revenue men, neither, otherwise your mother will be sorry to 'ear of your unfortunate accident. I 'ope I've made meself clear. Good day to ye, sir.' Jory tapped a couple of fingers to his forehead in a mocking salute before walking out of the door.

A furious and speechless Peter watched him go.

'He's right, sir, there's a lot more of them than us,' Richards said.

'Who are they, do you know?'

'Well, not really, sir. John the footman helps get barrels down to the cellar. Mostly so he can make sure nothing else in the cellar gets touched. I don't get involved because I'm too old and not strong enough. I think some of them who move the goods up here from the jetty are farm lads.

'As for the rest of them, I expect they are fishermen since boats are needed. I couldn't give you names because I don't know and I haven't wanted to be looking too closely at them in the half dark, either.'

There was a knock at the open door.

'Excuse me, sir, there's a gentleman called Baines here to see you. Says he's come from Lord Morton,' John said.

Peter hoped Baines was a steward who was here to lend him a hand, not to bring bad news from his father. He already had enough trouble for one day.

'Richards, see to Baines and ask Mrs Needham to find him a room if necessary. John, get in here and close the door.'

Richards left the room, John came in and shut the door.

'John, I understand you have helped the smugglers in the past.'

'Yes, sir, but only to keep the cellar properly organised and to make sure none of them help themselves to whatever else is in there.'

'Very well. I am determined to put a stop to the use of my cellars, although I'm not sure how yet how to do it. If you want to keep your post here, you make sure to remember you work for me, not the smugglers. Is this clear?'

'Yes, sir, and I don't want to get into trouble of any sort.'

'Stay on our side and I'll vouch for you if the authorities come around. Don't tell anybody what we might or might not be doing in the house, but if you hear of any plans from outsiders, you tell me and nobody else. Clear?'

'Yes, sir, understood.'

'I was going to be hiring a few more servants anyway. Now they'll even the numbers up against these smugglers, but I hear there are some farm lads who lend them a hand. Do you know who they are?'

John hesitated. Peter thought he did know, but didn't want to get anyone in trouble.

'Look, I only want to tell them to stay out of the way, so they don't help this Jory person. In fact, why don't you tell them instead of me? Then I don't need to know their names. Just remember you're helping me, not Jory.

'Besides, if I'm hiring another footman, you want to be first footman, not second footman or even a dismissed footman, isn't that so?'

John's eyes widened. Peter could see he hadn't considered the case of one of the new hires being another footman, or even his replacement. Peter wanted to be sure John understood where his best prospects lay.

'Well, sir, I expect I can find the right lads for a chat next time I'm down at the Blue Lion.'

'Good, you do that, and as soon as you can. Now go and find this Baines person when Richards or Mrs Needham are done with him and tell him I want to see him in here as soon as convenient.'

★ ★ ★

'Good morning, Mr Baines, please take a seat. Your name sounds familiar to me, but I can't think why.'

His appearance was vaguely recognisable, too. Baines was a young man, about the same age as Peter and with distinctive sandy-coloured hair. He had a strong feeling he had seen the hair before, but not on this man.

'Good morning, my lord. Perhaps you are thinking of my father, who is the land steward on the Northamptonshire estate. I have here a letter of introduction. I understand you are in need of a house and land steward.

'I have been assisting my father for some time and I think both he and the marquess thought it time I broadened my experience.'

It all fell into place for Peter. He had asked his father for some experienced help and here it was. It seemed his father really was willing to give him a fighting chance, now Peter had found out what had been going wrong at Ermcombe. Peter skimmed the letter quickly.

'Good. The previous steward here was a crook and robbed both the people and the estate of a great deal of money,' he said to Baines.

'I shall show you later what he was doing. My father says he is lending you to me for the remainder of this quarter. I should explain that he has given me this quarter to return the estate to profitability. If I do so, the estate will become mine.

'If we succeed, you will have a permanent post here as steward, should you wish it. If we don't, you may be going home as assistant to your father again and I may be taking ship to America.

'It would seem to me, Baines, we both have an incentive to get this place sorted out.'

'I look forward to the challenge, my lord. It seems we both have something to prove to our respective fathers.'

'Excellent. In the meantime, another problem has arisen. Smith, the steward, was involved with a band of smugglers. I have told them I want nothing more to do with them. Apart from anything else, you may imagine how my father would view it when he is a member of the government.

'However, just before you arrived, I was rudely informed the trade would continue making use of our cellars, by force if necessary. I need to consider what to do about it and I dare say you may want to rest after your journey. I shall see you at dinner, when we can discuss it.'

'Very good, my lord,' Baines said, rising and shaking the hand which was held out to him.

* * *

Peter remained at his desk, thinking everything over. Early tomorrow he would go with Baines around the handful of tenant farms to introduce him. Then he needed to go into Plymouth and look for men to hire. Hopefully, anyone he found wouldn't have any connection to the smugglers.

In view of Jory's threats, he might hire one or two more than he had intended. Out-of-work soldiers would be best as they would know how to fight, and it might come to that.

While he was there, he should speak to the Revenue men, too. It was risky in view of Jory's threat and Peter did value his life. However, the smuggling couldn't continue.

Furthermore, he could see it wouldn't be enough merely to scare or fight off the smugglers. He needed them caught.

He would let it be known he was hiring more men from Plymouth, but he wouldn't say to anyone he was visiting His Majesty's Customs and Excise. He wouldn't want the knowledge accidentally getting back to Jory.

He shook his head. His visit to Devon was proving far more dramatic than he had envisaged.

Plans Take Shape

Peter rode into Plymouth to visit the Preventive Officer first, before seeking some new employees. He left his horse at the Mayflower Inn and walked around to the Customs House. There was a uniformed officer in the entrance room who looked up as Peter walked in.

'Good morning, sir. I am Captain Lennon. How may I help you?'

'Good morning. May we speak in private?'

'Of course, sir,' the captain said. 'Come into my office, we will not be overheard there.'

He led Peter into an office at the back and closed the door behind them.

'Now, sir, what is it you want to speak about?'

'I am Lord Peter Wilson, son of the Marquess of Morton.'

The captain stood a little straighter.

'I have newly taken up residence on Lord Morton's Ermcombe Estate about ten miles east of here. I discovered the steward had been cheating everybody and was also in league with a band of smugglers. The steward is long gone, but the smugglers remain and have threatened violence if I don't allow them to use my cellars for storage. I am determined to stop them.'

'I'm glad to hear it, my lord, there are too many along this coast who turn a blind eye and make it difficult for us to do our duty. I am supposing you want us to catch them red-handed so there is no doubt they are guilty?'

'Exactly so. It will not be enough to stop the trade; the smugglers must be removed and my servants are unable to do much. I need to find more servants in any case — ideally ex-soldiers, who will also provide some muscle and fighting ability against the smugglers. I'm hoping you can suggest where I might find such men.'

'Certainly, sir. When you leave the building, turn left and continue down the quay until you find the Anchor. I dare say you'll find the men you need inside.'

'Good. Now, the estate is an hour's ride from here. If I send a message when the smugglers turn up, by the time you arrive the smugglers will be long gone. I am going to ask one of my tenant farmers to accommodate some of your men in one of their barns overnight so they are within easy reach. How many men do you have?'

'Only half a dozen Light Dragoons to cover forty miles of coastline. I could do with many more, but my superiors seem to consider it enough. I think they expect the Navy and the Water Guard to stop most of the trade.'

Captain Lennon sounded bitter. Peter supposed it was a thankless task, but there weren't a lot of options for a captain now the war with France was over. At least he wasn't on half-pay and perhaps Peter could provide him with an opportunity for some success.

'I don't know how many men the smugglers have, but if I can deny them help from my farms, find some ex-soldiers to hire and you can provide all your dragoons, I imagine it might be sufficient.'

'Do you know when they are expected?'

'Their leader said 'next week'. Do you have any idea when the moon and tide might suit them?'

'Just a moment, I have an almanac here with tides and phases of the moon.'

Captain Lennon fetched a book down from a shelf and opened it at the page marked by a ribbon. Clearly it was not the first time he had consulted the book for this information.

'Let me see,' he said, reaching for a sheet of paper and a pencil, 'we are fifteen minutes west of London and high tide is about four hours after Greenwich. I can get a more exact time from the Navy office, but this will do for now.

'I assume Ermcombe is on the river Erme and they may not want a full moon. Thus I would estimate next Monday or Tuesday night about ten p.m. as most likely.'

'This gives us most of a week to prepare. I shall go to the Anchor and see whom I can find. Once I have agreement from one of my tenants to use their barn, I'll return so we can finalise arrangements.'

'Very good, sir. Say to your farmer we shall arrive well after dark on Sunday and then stay under cover all day as well. We don't want anyone to know we are there, so as to keep an element of surprise for the smugglers.

'We won't need anything from the farmer, except to keep people away from his barn. We shall take everything we need with us.'

'Fine. I expect to be back on Thursday.'

Peter left and headed down the quay to the Anchor. As he went in, the noise subsided for a moment as men turned to see who it was. He was clearly of no great interest, as they soon turned back to their beers and conversation. Peter went up to the bar and the landlord came to serve him.

'A pint of your best, if you please,' Peter said.

He glanced around the pub as the landlord drew the beer. The mug was put on the bar and Peter put a shilling next to it. The landlord went to give him change, but Peter waved it away. He was more interested in information.

'I'm looking to hire some ex-soldiers. Do you know who might be interested?'

As he pocketed the coin, the landlord pursed his lips and looked around the bar.

'See the man in the brown coat and blue neckcloth by the fireplace?'

Peter nodded.

'Sergeant Cooper. He knows them all and can set you right.'

Peter took his beer over to the sergeant's table.

'Sergeant Cooper, Lord Peter Wilson. I'm looking for some ex-soldiers to hire. I'm told you're the man to speak to.'

Cooper looked Peter up and down with an assessing eye.

'Is this for a single task? Or permanent

jobs? And what sort of man would you be looking for, my lord?'

'I need a groom, ideally one who could become my stable master. I also need a footman, a gatekeeper, a couple of gardeners and a handyman who can fix windows, fences and the like.'

'So why are you looking for ex-soldiers?'

Cooper cocked his head to one side and squinted a little at Peter.

Peter had the feeling he was being interviewed for the post of employer.

'Why? Because there might be some trouble next week, so I need men who know how to fight if need be.

'Besides, I know there are a lot of men the army doesn't need any more, now Napoleon has been beaten.'

'Ah,' Cooper said, then sipped his beer. 'I do know a few who might suit you and could do with the work.'

'Good,' Peter said. 'Have another beer on me.'

He put a half-crown on to the table and Cooper's eyebrows rose before he slipped it into his pocket.

'I'm going around to the Mayflower now and taking their private parlour. Send them to me in the next couple of hours, if you will, and I'll speak to them there.'

'Very good, my lord,' Cooper said, saluting Peter with a finger to his forehead. 'I'll tell them to get there sharpish like.'

Peter nodded. He left his beer on the table for whoever wanted it and headed for the door. He wanted to speak in private to anyone who was interested, because it was better to surprise the smugglers rather than forewarning them.

He hadn't thought to reserve the parlour at the Mayflower, but it was unoccupied anyway. He ordered a Cornish pasty, coffee and writing materials. They had only just arrived when there was a knock on the door.

'Come!'

A head appeared in the opening.

'Are you the gentleman looking to hire ex-soldiers, sir?'

'Yes, come in and take a seat. What's your name?'

'Andrew Morris, my lord, corporal, Twenty-eighth Foot, late of the Gloucestershire Regiment, sir.'

Peter looked him over. He was young, but tall, fairly well spoken and appeared to be reasonably fit.

'How would you like to be a footman?'

'Very much, sir. There's not much work around here at the moment and my mother finds it hard to make ends meet. Father didn't come back from Trafalgar.'

'I should warn you there may be trouble next week from smugglers. They want to use my cellars and I plan to stop them. How would you feel about fighting them off if necessary?'

'If it comes to a fight I can handle it, sir. Will we have weapons?'

'A good question. I will see what can be provided. Very well, you're hired as second footman reporting to Mr Richards the butler.

'The pay is two pounds a quarter, plus full board. We'll worry about a livery for you later. Be back here at noon on Thursday and I'll arrange transport to Ermcombe.'

Peter put a coin on the table.

'You'll get paid at the end of the quarter. In the meantime, here is half a crown. You might want to give half of that to your mother.'

'Thank you, sir,' the new footman said, taking the coin and standing. 'I'll do so.'

'To make a start on your new duties, you can stand outside the door here. If anyone else comes, you can send them in to me, one at a time.'

Peter made a note on the sheet of paper whom he had hired, for which post and the pay he had stated. He then added a reminder for himself to arrange a wagon for Thursday and get some weapons. He would ask Captain Lennon if there were some he could borrow.

Soon afterwards, there was a knock at the door and Andrew poked his head in.

'Sergeant Cooper to see you, sir.'

'Very good, send him in.'

Peter wondered if Cooper was going

to tell him about more men he could hire or if he wanted a job himself.

The door opened wider and Cooper came in, walking with a pronounced limp.

'Sergeant Cooper, I hadn't expected to see you again quite so soon.'

'Well, my lord, I wondered if you could take me on as a groom. As you can see, I took a ball in the knee at Waterloo and it's left me with a permanent limp, but I know my way around a horse and can still ride.'

'Take a seat and tell me about yourself. Were you a groom before?'

'I was a farrier for the Royal Horse Guards, my lord. Nobody in Plymouth needs a farrier that doesn't already have one.'

'A farrier! And for the Horse Guards! Good heavens, I think I need you for my stable master.'

Cooper grinned in relief.

Peter could see Cooper was going to cost him more than a groom, but if a small forge was set up beside his stable,

Cooper could shoe the tenant farmers' horses as well as maintain the stable.

Not only that, but once they had their own forge, Cooper could make and repair all sorts of estate equipment, too. It might not cost him anything in the long run.

'Excellent. I only have one groom at the moment, and he's not the brightest of fellows so I'll be glad to have someone else take charge.

'I'll need a waggon to take everybody to Ermcombe on Thursday. I'm sure you know your way around Plymouth, so I'll leave you to organise it. The driver can be paid on arrival if I don't see him before.'

'Thank you, sir, I'll get on with it straight away,' Cooper said and limped his way to the door.

Peter was feeling positive. The Preventive Officer was co-operative and it looked like he had found two good men so far.

Then, within the next hour, he found himself an ex-sailor with a wooden leg for a gatekeeper; a couple of muscular ex-army privates to be gardeners and finally, a ship's carpenter for his handyman.

He decided to call upon Captain Lennon once more about weapons. There seemed little point in actually buying them. Firstly, he hoped they would only be needed once. Secondly, he couldn't spare the money.

Thirdly, if he was helping the captain to stop smuggling, it seemed reasonable for the captain to help him. He walked around to the Custom House again.

'My lord, did you manage to find some suitable men?'

'Yes, thank you for your suggestion. However, if we are to put up some stern resistance to the smugglers, we need to borrow weapons from you.'

'What did you have in mind? If there is to be close fighting, I don't think muskets or rifles would suit. Too slow to reload.'

'I wondered about half a dozen sabres and pistols. Would they be possible?'

The captain rubbed his chin thoughtfully.

'Sabres might be a problem; we only have a couple to spare. However, sword bayonets might do just as well. I'll ask the Captain of Marines if he can lend us some, and pistols, too.'

'Good, I shall be back on Thursday to tell you which barn can be used.'

★ ★ ★

Before Peter headed back, he went around to the bootmaker to collect his new dancing slippers. As he rode home, Peter was feeling very pleased about life. It had been a very satisfactory day. Living down here in Devon was a lot more invigorating than he would ever have imagined.

He saw little reason he wouldn't be able to sort out the estate woes with the assistance of Baines. Also, he now had an appropriate number of servants to renovate the house, gardens and stables. Given the new servants and help from the dragoons, he should be able to put a stop to the smuggling as well.

The sun was dropping in the sky as he neared home, so he and his horse threw a long shadow in front of themselves. Tomorrow, he and Baines needed to visit the farms to find a suitable barn. Tomorrow as well, he was going to give a second lesson in the waltz to a pretty young lady.

Yes, life in Devon was working out far better than he had expected.

The Last Waltz?

Peter and Baines rode around the farms, to find a barn for the dragoons. It was still early in the year, so they were not expecting to find any of the barns full. They noticed Tomas's farm had a very large barn in his farmyard and rode in. As they entered, Mr Tomas came out to meet them.

'Good morning, my lord, Mr Baines.'

'Good morning, Mr Tomas,' Peter said, dismounting, 'we are looking for someone with a large barn which has space for some temporary storage.'

'Storage, my lord?' the farmer asked, as one of his boys ran up to hold the horses.

'Yes, it is a confidential matter. Might we see inside the barn?' Peter asked.

'Yes of course, my lord, but I tell you now, I don't wanna have nothing to do with contraband goods. I know some folks hereabouts think it's all right, but I don't hold with illegal activities myself.

'Besides, these freetraders as they call 'emselves, they're a lot of ruffians and ne'er-do-wells what I don't want to have no truck with. Smith robbed us afore and I willn't rob nobody else, not even the government, not even when we don't agree with 'em taxes. It's a question of self respect. I hope you're not gonna ask me for summat what I can't do, beggin' your pardon, milord, even after you reduced the rent an' all.'

'I'm very glad to hear it, Mr Tomas. I don't want to trouble your conscience. I'm trying to stop the smugglers making free with the cellars of Ermcombe House, because I have much the same opinion of them as you.

'What I need is somewhere to hide a half dozen light dragoons for a couple of days. I wondered if we could use your barn? Naturally I would compensate you for the inconvenience and pay for hay used by their horses, for example.'

'Dragoons, you say?'

'Yes, we're expecting the smugglers to show up next Monday or Tuesday night.

We need somewhere for the dragoons to hide, nearby, but out of sight. Once the smugglers appear the dragoons have to be able to turn up quickly and arrest them.

'If they can hide in your barn I can get word to them and have them at Ermcombe House within twenty minutes, soon enough to catch them red-handed.'

By this time, they had wandered across to the large stone barn. Tomas pulled the door wide and they went in. It was mostly empty except for some straw and hay.

'As you see, sir, there's plenty of room. Later in the year I hope it'll be filling up, but I doubts the harvest will be good this year. It's much colder than it ought by now and if'n the weather don't warm up soon, it'll be a poor year.'

'Looks perfect to me, Mr Tomas. Baines here will see you about compensation after the dragoons have left. Naturally, nobody else should know about this, as we don't want to tip off the smugglers. Make sure your wife, children and farmhands say nothing.'

'Of course not, my lord. If I might suggest the dragoons come on Sunday af'rnoon while everybody's at church? Then they've a chance of arriving without anybody seeing them riding around these 'ere parts.'

'Good thinking, Mr Tomas. I'll get Baines to meet them on the road from Plymouth and show them where to go.'

'There should be no problem with me meeting the dragoons, my lord,' Baines said as they headed home, 'nobody has seen me at church yet, so nobody will miss me.'

Peter consulted his pocket watch.

'Time we were heading back. I am due at Harford House at eleven.'

Arriving a few minutes before eleven o'clock, Peter could hear a waltz tune being played as he changed his riding boots for dancing slippers.

As it stopped and then restarted, he realised it must be Anne memorising it, although he wasn't sure who was playing it, her or Mr Healey. Gerrard escorted him up to the music room.

'Good morning, ladies, Mr Healey,' he said with a bow.

He noticed the furniture, other than the piano, had been pushed right back against the walls and the carpet had been rolled up to the far end as well.

Mr Healey stopped playing and bowed to him, while Lady Hermione gave him a nod. Anne, however, sprang from a second piano stool and quickly made her way around the piano.

'Lord Peter, you are here,' she said, stating the obvious.

She held out her hand, and Peter raised it to his lips. She started a little in surprise. He supposed she had been expecting him to simply hold her hand or perhaps even to draw her straight into a waltz hold.

However, by the little smile on her face, he didn't think she had minded at all. Lady Hermione interrupted his thoughts.

'Lord Peter, shall we get on with the

lesson at once? I have ordered refreshments for an hour's time.'

'Of course,' he said, but then looked down at Anne's feet.

Light blue embroidered slippers peeped out below a matching light blue empire line dress with embroidered hem and neckline.

'I see you have new dancing slippers, Miss Harford; are they comfortable?'

'Yes indeed, sir. I heard a rumour you were to get new dancing slippers, too.'

'That is correct, but alas, mine are very plain and not as attractive as yours.'

'Lord Peter,' Lady Hermione said, 'if we may get started?'

Peter cleared his throat and lifted Anne's hand, which he had not released. Without hesitating, Anne put her left hand on his shoulder. It was his turn to be a little surprised, as she had obviously remembered his height and thus where to find his shoulder.

'So,' he said, 'let us try the reverse turn.'

Within the hour Anne had learned the

reverse turn, how to promenade in the waltz and how to deal with changes of speed. By the end of the lesson the two of them were waltzing around the whole room to a complete piece of music played by Mr Healey.

'Bravo, Anne,' Lady Hermione said, 'I was most impressed. Nobody would ever know you cannot see where you are going.'

'I have a very good teacher in Lord Peter,' Anne said, 'and I was quite sure we would not crash into anything, so thank you, my lord.'

'The pleasure was all mine,' he said. 'I think it only remains now for us to be on the alert for a suitable assembly where there is to be waltzing.'

He reflected it really had been a pleasure and he had thoroughly enjoyed dancing with her. Much more, in fact, than he had ever enjoyed dancing in the past.

Unfortunately she had learned too quickly for there to be an excuse for another lesson, which was a great pity.

Anne was a bit breathless with all the twirling around the room. She couldn't remember when she had enjoyed herself so much and didn't want it to end. But it had to end, and then she was aching to know when they might dance again. In the meantime, Peter had escorted her to the dining-room where they had a light meal in the company of her aunt and Mr Healey.

When he left, Peter had kissed her fingers again and she went bubbling upstairs to tell Mabel all about it.

Danger on the Horizon

'All the servants are assembled in the entrance hall, sir,' Richards said.

Peter went out of his study to the hall and then a few steps up the stairs. This way he could see them all and they could all see him.

'I've called you all here because we have some new members of staff and you need to be able to recognise each other. When we've finished here, you can all go down to the servants' hall where Cook has a meal for you. This includes all the outside servants who would normally eat in their own accommodation.

'Now, as you all know, there is a band of smugglers who are insisting on using our cellars to store their contraband. However, the estate is owned by my father, the Marquess of Morton, who is a member of the government and thus opposed to smuggling.

'If he learns his estate is involved in smuggling, then all of us will be in big trouble, myself included. Therefore we have to put a stop to it. The smugglers say they are going to use our cellars and will do so by force if necessary.

'I expect them to arrive on next Monday or Tuesday night, but we will be ready for them. All you men will have a pistol and sword bayonet each. I am hoping they will realise there are too many of us now and we're armed as well, so they'll give up without a fight and go elsewhere.'

Peter had decided not to mention the dragoons, nor his intention to catch the smugglers. If he did, there was a chance careless talk would find its way back to Jory and his plan would fail.

'Since many of you don't know each other and it will be half dark, you will each be given a neckerchief to wear. The housekeeper, Mrs Needham and her maids will make a yellow one for each of you, which you will be given on Sunday evening or Monday morning.

'This way you should be able to tell the difference between yourselves and the smugglers when it's almost dark. I don't want any of you shooting one another because of mistaken identity.

'You are to wear these from Monday onwards but only while you are on estate grounds. We don't want the smugglers finding out and getting yellow neckerchiefs for themselves. Any questions?'

A hand went up.

'Yes, Cooper?'

'Are you going to wear one as well, sir?'

It was a very good question, and it hadn't occurred to Peter to tell Mrs Needham he would need one as well.

'I certainly will. Make a note, Mrs Needham, everybody is to have one without exception. I certainly don't want any of you shooting me by mistake,' he said, frowning at them all.

There was a chuckle from many of the group.

'Good, welcome to Ermcombe, and now go downstairs to enjoy your meal.'

★   ★   ★

On Sunday, as Peter made his way up the aisle of the church, he noticed his new servants were there, too. By the murmurs from the rest of the congregation, there was some speculation about them. As he made his way in to the aristocratic pews he saw Anne listening intently, probably wondering what was going on.

'Good morning, Lord Peter,' Anne said. 'Will you sit with us?'

'Good morning, ladies. Yes, thank you,' he said.

Peter wondered how Anne knew it was him, unless it was just an intelligent guess. He sat next to her.

'Lord Peter,' Anne said quietly, 'what is everybody talking about?'

'I imagine they are discussing the new faces in the congregation. I have employed six new servants because the estate was hopelessly understaffed. They are ex-soldiers and sailors from Plymouth, so unknown to the people here.

'The previous week I employed a new housemaid, but she was a local girl so she didn't generate any particular interest or speculation.'

Peter gazed over the congregation as the vicar ascended to the pulpit and started speaking. Peter only recognised a few faces; most were a mystery to him. He couldn't see Jory, but he wondered if some faces were Jory's fellow smugglers. He then wondered if those fellow smugglers had wives and children.

If the men were caught by the dragoons and then hanged or transported, it would be very hard for their families. Still, if they weren't caught by the dragoons, they always ran the risk of being caught by the Water Guard or Royal Navy ships. They knew the risks and Peter had little choice in the matter.

He hoped, for the sake of their families, they might recognise the trade was now hopeless.

Kidnapped!

Everybody had dined and there was a certain listlessness in the air. They were all waiting to see if anything was going to happen.

Shortly after nine o'clock, Peter heard the front door open and Richards protesting about something. Rapid footsteps came down the tiled hall and the study door was suddenly thrust open so that it banged against the wall. Peter stood and faced the doorway to see a smirking Jory.

'There you are, me lord,' Jory said. 'I think you must have not been listening or not taken me seriously last time we spoke.

'Everybody knows you've hired a handful of ex-soldiers, but them won't be enough to stop us. But we don't want anyone gettin' hurt, do we? So we've done somethin' else to make sure you and your servants step aside.

'Yer little friend Miss Harford, the blind girl, isn't home right now. We've put her somewhere else for the time being. Now provided you co-operate, she'll be home for breakfast, none the worse. If you don't keep out of our way, you won't be seeing her again.'

'You devil!' Peter growled, starting around the desk.

'Ah, ah, ah!' Jory said, wagging a finger. 'You touch me and you willn't see your little friend again, so keep yer distance. And it's no good a'calling the Revenue tomorrow about barrels in yer cellar, cos we'll put it about how yer in charge of the smuggling — even if you don't have an unfortunate little accident soon after.'

Peter scowled at Jory, his fists clenched. He wanted to beat Jory to a pulp for involving Anne.

'I see yer understanding me now, my lord, so you sit down and enjoy some of yer fine French brandy, while I go about me business.' He tapped a couple of fingers to his forehead in a mocking salute again, before walking out of the door.

Peter listened to Jory's boots tapping on the tiles as he walked unhurriedly to the front door. Richards appeared at the study door, waiting for orders while Peter considered what to do.

'John,' he said to one of the footmen standing behind Richards, 'run to the stables and tell Cooper to get my and Mr Baines's horses ready.'

'Andrew,' he said to his new second footman, 'find Mr Baines and bring him to me at once.'

'Richards, assemble the men and make sure they are each wearing their yellow neckcloth and have their weapons to hand.'

Peter ran upstairs to his room where Frederick was waiting with his riding gear and the yellow neckerchief. He put a loaded pistol into each of his coat pockets. When he came back down, Baines was waiting in the hall.

'Baines, I have to go to Harford House. Jory says he has taken Miss Harford. Go to Tomas's Farm and rouse the dragoons. When you get back, you are in charge until I return. If you can, hold the smugglers back from the house until the dragoons come up behind them. Don't start a fight unless you must.'

Peter galloped to Harford House where he leapt off his horse and pounded on the front door until he could hear the bolts being slid back. As the door started to open he pushed it wide, to find Gerrard was there.

'Gerrard, is Miss Anne here?'

'As far as I am aware, my lord, she is abed,' a frowning Gerrard said.

'We must check, I've been told she has been abducted,' Peter said, racing up the stairs two at a time.

As he reached the second landing, he realised he didn't know which was Anne's bedroom, so he paused and waited for Gerrard, who wasn't far behind, to catch up. He saw the housekeeper was hot on his heels too. They were both holding candlesticks and shielding the flames with their other hand. They arrived at the second door in the hallway and Gerrard paused.

'Mrs Carlow,' Gerrard said, pointing to the door, 'take a look, please.'

The housekeeper went past him and opened the door. She had taken no more than a step inside before she screamed.

Gerard and Peter pushed past her to see there was a girl on the floor with hands and feet tied, and a sack over her head. She was making muffled noises and drumming her heels on the floor.

'Miss Anne!' Mrs Carlow cried and dropped to her knees beside the girl.

Gerrard went around the room lighting other candles.

Peter was confused. He had expected Anne to be missing, not tied up and left on the floor in her room. The housekeeper pulled the sack off the girl's head and he saw it wasn't Anne, it was her maid instead. He looked around quickly, saw the bed was empty and Anne wasn't anywhere here.

'Where is Miss Anne?' he asked Mabel, as Mrs Carlow removed a gag from the maid's mouth.

In reply Mabel burst into tears and sobbed violently until the housekeeper smacked her cheek.

'Calm down,' Mrs Carlow said, 'and tell us what's happened to Miss Anne.'

Mabel looked reproachfully at the housekeeper and hiccuped a couple of times. Gerrard sat her up and started untying the cord holding Mabel's hands behind her back.

'I heard a noise like Miss Anne yelping in surprise,' Mabel said, 'so I came in to see what had happened. I thought maybe she'd knocked into a chair or something. Then someone pushed me to the floor, gagged me and tied my hands. I think there were two men. It was almost dark and they put the bag over my head, so then I couldn't see anyway.

'It sounded like Miss Anne was struggling and then they went out and closed the door behind them. I couldn't do anything because they tied my feet as well.'

Peter, Gerrard and Mrs Carlow looked at each other. Peter saw he was right, she had been abducted.

'What time was this?' he asked.

'A half hour or so. I heard Miss Anne's clock striking,' Mabel said.

'Not long after they went up,' Gerrard said.

'You didn't see them, so they must have gone down the back stairs,' Peter said.

'I don't know how they got in,' Gerrard said, 'I made sure all the doors were locked and bolted.'

'Let's have a look,' Peter said, ' just in case it's a bluff and she's still in the house.'

He waved Gerrard in front of him and they hurried down the stairs. The outside door at the bottom was closed but unlocked and unbolted.

'I swear . . .' Gerrard started, but Peter waved him to silence.

'Yes, I'm sure it was locked, but somebody unlocked it, the question is, where have they gone?'

Peter thought for a moment while the others looked to him to take charge and tell them what to do.

'Where is Robbie, her dog?'

'In his basket in my parlour,' Mrs Carlow said.

182

'Bring him here if you please and send a housemaid up to Mabel. Gerrard, her ladyship needs to be made aware, then send the footmen down to help search the grounds.'

They hurried off while Peter waited by the door. He wondered where they might have taken her.

He hadn't seen anyone on the road here and he guessed they wouldn't have gone far in half an hour, anyway. Certainly not if they intended to return her as soon as his cellars had been filled.

He supposed Baines and Captain Lennon were dealing with the smugglers back at Ermcombe. At this point he didn't care much about them; all he cared about was Anne. She must be terrified out of her wits. When he caught those two men he was going to kill them for what they had done. Just then Mrs Carlow returned with Robbie on a simple lead.

'Robbie, sit,' Peter said, and the dog sat in front of him.

Peter unclipped his lead.

'Robbie, where is Anne? Smell, Robbie, smell. Find Anne, Robbie, find Anne,' Peter said, opening the door.

Was this dog as clever as Peter hoped? Robbie looked at him for a moment before standing and sniffing around. Then he went out of the door, with his nose to the ground following a trail. Peter hoped he was following his mistress's scent, not the kitchen cat or something else irrelevant.

Peter followed the dog. Robbie went several hundred yards out into the grounds before suddenly coming to a halt.

'Gerrof, gerrout of 'ere,' a threatening voice came from the dark.

Robbie growled.

'Clear orf, I say,' the voice said and a man stepped forward holding a cudgel which he swung at Robbie.

Robbie barked and dodged sideways as Peter stepped forward and punched the man hard in the face. The man fell back and then to the ground. Peter could hear people coming behind him and looked around to see it was Gerrard and one of the footmen.

'It's the ice house,' Gerrard said.

Peter stepped over the man, leaving the others to deal with him, to see the door of the ice house had a bar across the door.

'Robbie! Robbie!' Anne called from inside and the dog barked again.

Peter lifted the bar and tossed it to the side before pulling the door open.

'Anne, my love,' Peter said, 'you're safe now.'

Anne flung herself at Peter who caught her and held her tightly. She was shivering. Peter didn't know if it was from fright or the cold of the ice house. She put her arms around his neck.

'Peter.' She sobbed. 'You came for me. I was so frightened, I didn't know if I was ever going to get out of there.'

'You're safe now. Let me get you to the house so you can warm up.'

He put his hand under her knees and swung her up into his arms. As he passed the man on the ground, he kicked him hard in the ribs. Ordinarily he wouldn't kick a man while he was down, but he would have liked to do much more if he didn't have a freezing cold girl in his arms.

'What shall we do with this one, my lord?' Gerrard asked.

'Put him in the ice house, we can deal with him later,' Peter said, not pausing in his stride towards the house.

They entered the house by the kitchen door and as the kitchen was very warm, he thought to stay there for the moment. However, looking around, he saw the servant's hall was adjacent and had more space, so went in there instead. He sat in one of the chairs, with Anne still cradled in his arms. Robbie had followed them and now sat beside them, looking up at his mistress.

'Bring a blanket,' Peter said to one of the maids hovering nearby, 'and alert Lady Hermione.' Then he looked down at the dog. 'Robbie, you are a good dog, a very, very good dog.'

Robbie wagged his tail.

'Robbie found me?' Anne asked.

'Yes. We didn't know where you had been taken, so I told Robbie to find you and I just followed him.'

Just then Lady Hermione came into the servants' hall followed by Mrs Carlow, Gerrard and seemingly all the maids, footmen and gardeners, too. Mabel stepped closer and then hesitated, seeing Anne still in Peter's arms and not sure at first what to do. She took the blanket from one of the chambermaids and wrapped it around Anne.

'My goodness,' Lady Hermione said, 'what on earth has happened?'

'A band of smugglers is trying to force my hand by abducting Miss Harford and threatening dire consequences for her if I don't co-operate,' Peter said.

'I'd left Miss Anne to drink her milk while I went put things away in the dressing-room. I heard a noise and thought she had bumped into something so I went to see.

'There were two men in Miss Anne's bedchamber. They tied me up and took

Miss Anne away,' Mabel added.

As Lady Hermione was being given a slightly disjointed account of the following events, Peter was reminded there had been two men, one of whom was now bruised and in the ice house. Also the outside door had been opened from the inside. He hadn't seen the other.

'One moment,' Peter said loudly, causing everyone else to fall silent. 'One of the men is in the ice house, but where is the second man?'

'It was Walter,' Anne said, quite distinctly.

Everyone's eyes turned to Walter, who was one of the footmen.

'No, it wasn't,' he said, 'it wasn't me. How can she say it was me when she can't see who it was?'

'Because, Walter, I recognised your smell,' Anne said.

'Recognised my smell? No, it's ridiculous, it's nonsense, how can you recognise someone by their smell?' Walter asked.

'It was definitely you, Walter, I have no doubt,' Anne said calmly.

Walter licked his lips and looked around the room at everybody who was now staring at him. He made a sudden dash for the door, but Joseph stepped into the opening, blocked his way and tussled with Walter to stop him escaping. Gerrard came up, grabbed Walter's arm and twisted it up behind his back.

'I think we know now who opened the outside door and let his partner in crime into the house,' Gerrard said. 'It's into the cellar for you, my lad, until the magistrate gets here.'

'No,' Peter said, with a snarl, 'why don't you put him in the ice house with the other one? See how he likes it.'

'But I'll freeze in the ice house,' Walter said.

'Pity you didn't think of that when you put Miss Anne in there,' Gerrard said.

He pushed Walter towards the doorway.

'You gardeners go as well, please,' Peter said. 'We don't want anyone getting away.'

'Jane,' Mrs Carlow said, 'run up to

Miss Anne's room and get a good fire going. Elsie, go up as well and clean up any spilt milk, then bring the cup down. Doris, take a warming pan and a hot brick upstairs too.'

'I'll warm up some more milk,' the cook said.

'Lord Peter,' Lady Hermione said, 'thank you for your help. I think Mabel and I should get Anne back upstairs and into a warm bed.'

Peter was suddenly very conscious he was sitting there in the servants' hall cuddling a young lady. A young lady who was wearing nothing more than her night rail, dressing gown, a blanket and carpet slippers.

It was thoroughly improper, but nobody had seemed shocked or scandalised. However, the crisis was past now and proper standards had to be observed once more. This didn't stop him giving her a little squeeze and a kiss on her forehead.

'You're safe now,' he said to Anne quietly. 'Go to bed, sleep well and I'll see you tomorrow. Perhaps you could take Robbie upstairs with you as well, for reassurance.'

'Thank you for rescuing me, Peter,' she said equally quietly into his cravat, as she pressed her cheek to his chest.

She slipped off his lap and Mabel put an arm around her shoulders to guide her back upstairs.

'I must go back to Ermcombe and see what is happening,' he said to Lady Hermione. 'All being well, the band of smugglers have been caught by my staff and some dragoons, but I need to be there.'

'Thank you again, Lord Peter. We shall see you tomorrow.'

He went out to the front of the house to find his horse was still there, placidly eating grass from the lawn. Cantering home, he wondered what he would find when he got there. He patted his pockets to make sure he still had his pistols.

As he entered his drive, the gatekeeper was standing there, leaning on the gate and waiting for him. He straightened up as he recognised Peter.

'My lord,' he said, 'the dragoons passed half an hour ago and then I could hear shouting at the house and a few shots fired, too.'

'Very good. Close the gate now in case anyone tries to escape this way.'

Peter took one of the pistols from his pocket and started his horse trotting down the drive. He hadn't gone far when he saw a horse galloping towards him.

'Hold or I shoot!' he shouted.

In response there was a flash of a pistol and he felt a searing pain in the arm holding the reins. He convulsively gripped his pistol and was conscious of it going off as he felt himself spinning from his horse. The last thing he remembered was hitting the ground hard.

Fatal Shot

The next morning at Harford House was a busy one. The magistrate had arrived early and taken statements from Anne, Mabel and Gerrard. Then the shivering miscreants had been tied together and taken on foot to Plymouth, escorted by a couple of dragoons.

Anne now sat in her room, idly scratching Robbie behind his ear. She had a lot to think about after the events of the last 24 hours.

She recalled how shocked she had been to be grabbed, gagged and thrown across a man's shoulder. Anne shivered at how terrified she had been, not knowing what was going on nor where they were going.

She had known it was Walter carrying her and had wondered briefly if there was a fire and he was taking her to safety. The thought had been quickly dismissed because she hadn't heard any alarm and Walter hadn't spoken a single word to her.

Then, she had realised she had been put in the ice house and the door shut had been shut. If anything, it had been a relief, because at least she had known where she was and it didn't look as if she was going to be taken elsewhere. As to why she was there, she had had no idea at the time. And as they hadn't tied her hands, it was easy to remove her gag. She had been tempted to cry out, but had realised at once it was pointless.

Having gone to the trouble of shutting her in the ice house, they obviously wouldn't let her out just for the asking, and nobody else was likely to be close enough to hear her.

She had pressed an ear to the door, but it was very thick and she couldn't make out what they were saying.

After a while it went quiet and she had supposed one or both of them had gone away. As time passed, oh so slowly, she had started to get colder and colder. She had been dressed for bed in a night gown and a dressing gown, not dressed to go out on a cold night. She had known if she was left there long enough, she would surely freeze to death.

Hearing Robbie growling, barking and a man trying to scare him off had been a relief, but only for a moment, because then something had thumped against the door. She had been so worried Robbie had been hurt.

She remembered calling out, fearing for him, and being so happy to hear Robbie bark back to her and know it hadn't been him hitting the door. Then an instant later the door had opened and a familiar voice had said 'Anne, my love.'

Anne stopped running through last night's events in her mind to recall the moment again. Had he really called her his love? Yes, she was quite sure he had said it. Did he mean it? Or was it just careless speech in the heat of the moment? Whatever the case, she had been so glad to throw herself into the arms of her rescuer.

She remembered a story Mabel had read to her years ago about a princess trapped in a tower and guarded by a dragon. Then a handsome prince had come along, slain the dragon and rescued the princess.

Well, now she knew just how the princess must have felt. Her hero had carried her off, back to the house and into the very welcome warmth. She had felt safe and cared for, sitting on her hero's lap and with his arms holding her tightly.

It was like a dream that Peter had come to save her. She hadn't realised at first how many of the servants had been there to see her snuggling into his overcoat. Now she felt herself blushing, just thinking about it.

The servants' hall must be rife with speculation this morning, not just about her and Lord Peter, but about her kidnappers, too. She hoped Walter would get transported so she wouldn't ever meet him again.

And what had possessed him to help the smuggling gang? Anne wondered what had happened at Ermcombe last night. No doubt Lord Peter would tell them when he called this morning. She couldn't remember if she had thanked him properly, she had been so emotional after being rescued.

'Come along, Robbie, it's time we went down to the morning-room. I have to ask Aunt Hermione if I embarrassed everybody last night.'

She grasped Robbie's shoulder handle and headed for the door.

As she entered the morning-room, she heard her aunt exclaim in distress.

'Oh, no, Anne, Lord Peter has been injured. I've just had a note from his valet.'

'Injured? Badly?' Anne asked.

'It doesn't say, but I suppose his valet must have known he was planning to come this morning and so he sent the note.'

'If his valet sent it, Lord Peter must be unable to write himself, so he must be seriously hurt. We must go to him.'

'Yes, indeed,' Lady Hermione said, going to the bell pull, 'after what he has done for us, there is no doubt of it. Run upstairs and put on your boots and pelisse; we must go at once.'

When they arrived at Ermcombe, Anne wanted to hurry into the house, but could not, unfamiliar as she was with the entrance. She had to wait for her aunt to hand her down from the carriage and then guide her in through the door held open by Richards.

'Good morning, my lady, good morning Miss Harford,' he said.

'How is Lord Peter?' Lady Hermione asked.

'Asleep in bed, ma'am. We are waiting for the doctor to return this morning.'

'We must go up to him,' Anne said, who was full of anxiety to know how he was.

There was a pause, and Anne bit her bottom lip as she waited for someone to say something.

'Come, come, now,' Lady Hermione said, 'there cannot be any impropriety while I am escorting my niece and your master is asleep as well. Send up the housekeeper, too, if it makes you happier.'

'Very well, my lady, if you would come with me.'

Lady Hermione put her arm across Anne's shoulders to guide her as they followed the butler up the stairs. At Peter's room Richards opened the door a crack and looked in, before opening the door wide.

'Fredericks,' he said softly, 'Lady Hermione and Miss Harford are here to see his lordship.'

He stood aside to let the ladies enter and Fredericks rose from a chair beside the bed. Lady Hermione led Anne to the vacated chair and Anne put out her hand to find the bed. Her aunt took Anne's hand and placed it on top of Peter's hand which was resting on the bed cover.

'Tell us what happened, if you please,' Hermione said to Fredericks.

'It seems he was riding back home when he met the leader of the smuggling gang riding the other way up the drive. There was an exchange of shots and his lordship fell from his horse. The gatekeeper was nearby with a lantern and was able to bind his wound roughly before coming to the house for help.

'Unfortunately the gatekeeper was a sailor, so he does not ride. Also he has a wooden leg and cannot run very quickly, so it was a while before milord could be brought to the house and his injury tended to properly. He appears to have lost a lot of blood and has been unconscious since he was brought here.'

'What did the doctor say?'

'Captain Lennon, the Preventive Officer in charge of the dragoons had the foresight to send for the doctor before the smugglers arrived, so he was to hand. He thought milord had hit his head when he fell from his horse, as well as being shot in the arm.'

'And?' Lady Hermione said, lowering her voice.

'He thought his lordship should recover,' Fredericks said, equally quietly, 'provided infection doesn't take hold and the head injury isn't serious.

'The ball went completely through his arm without hitting the bone, which is why he lost so much blood. We have to wait and see how he does. The doctor will be back to see him again later today.'

'Has his father been informed?'

'No, milady. I was about to do so just as soon as someone came to relieve me and sit with him.'

Hermione glanced at Anne, who was looking miserable and caressing Lord Peter's hand.

'Miss Anne can look after him for a moment. Show me to a writing desk. I was intending to write to Lord Harford today and I shall write to Lord Morton at the same time. Anne, I shall not be long. We shall leave the door open, so call out if you need assistance.'

Anne solemnly nodded agreement.

After a thoughtful glance at her niece, Lady Hermione followed Fredericks out of the room.

Anne felt terrible. After saving her from freezing to death in the ice house, Peter had ridden home only to be shot. Now he was the one in danger of dying. Tears rolled down her cheeks.

'Oh Peter,' she said, and squeezed his hand gently, 'please don't die, I need you. You must get well, I want to dance with you again.'

Anne sobbed quietly and lifted his hand to her lips. As she did so, there was an answering feeble squeeze of her hand.

'Peter? Peter, are you awake?' 'Anne,' came an answering whisper. She slid her hand up his arm to find his face and caressed his cheek. He turned his head slightly to press gently into her hand. She heard someone coming down the corridor, so replaced her hand on his where it lay on the coverlet.

'Miss, would you care for a cup of tea?' a familiar voice asked.

'Fredericks, I think he may be waking.' She heard him come to the bed and supposed he was studying his master.

'It appears he may have gone back to sleep, miss, but if he is stirring, it's very welcome. I shall go and tell Cook to have some broth for when he does wake. The tea?'

'Yes, thank you.'

She heard him cross the room and then felt a cloth put into her other hand, before he left again. Anne felt the cloth with her thumb and finger. It appeared to be a man's handkerchief. Fredericks had obviously noticed her tear-stained cheeks, but was sufficiently thoughtful not to remark upon them.

She wiped her tears away and as she did so, noticed there was a monogram embroidered in a corner. She touched it carefully and realised it must be PW, Peter's initials. She wiped her eyes once again, then carefully tucked the hand-kerchief into her sleeve. More footsteps approached.

'Come, Anne,' Lady Hermione said, 'the doctor is here. We shall go to the breakfast-room for refreshments while he is with Lord Peter.'

★ ★ ★

A short while later Baines entered the breakfast-room. He was sporting a very large and vivid bruise on his face.

'Good morning, milady, I am Baines, the steward,' he said.

'Baines, good morning. I suppose from your large bruise you were involved in the incident last night?' Lady Hermione said.

'Yes, indeed. I understand from your groom Miss Harford was abducted by a couple of the smugglers and only released by the intervention of his lordship.'

'I am grateful to him for raising the alarm and then rescuing me,' Anne said. 'If not for Lord Peter, I might have been frozen to death by this morning. We were very distressed to hear he had been injured on his return. Have many people been hurt?'

'Mostly bruises and a few cuts, miss. Once the smugglers realised we were armed and the dragoons had arrived as well, they gave up. We caught four of them and probably the same number ran off.

'Since it was mostly dark and they ran away, it was impossible to follow them, but I doubt we will see them again. The leader, a man called Jory, jumped on his horse and rode away. It was he whom his lordship encountered in the driveway.'

'So the leader shot Lord Peter and then escaped?' Anne asked, sounding and feeling angry.

'Oh no, miss, his lordship must have shot him at the same time he was shot himself. We found Jory on the ground, quite dead from a bullet wound.'

Anne's hand shot to her mouth in horror. It could have been the other way around. She felt her aunt grasp her other hand.

'Don't be upset, Anne,' her aunt said 'Just know he can't hurt you or Lord Peter again.'

'No, it's not that. It's because it could so easily have been Peter lying dead on the ground.'

'But it wasn't and we must be thankful. I'm sure he will make a full recovery if he is already stirring.'

'My apologies,' Baines said, 'I had not wished to upset you, but I thought you should know everything since you have been involved.'

'You are correct. Do continue, Mr Baines,' Lady Hermione said.

'I have little to add. His lordship had prepared well, hoping to avoid as many injuries as possible. A dragoon is guarding the contraband until it can be confiscated by the Revenue officer. The remaining dragoons have taken the captured smugglers to Plymouth.

'I have written a full account for Lord Morton and have taken the liberty of enclosing your letters, all of which I am sending express today. I believe Lord Morton to be in London, but I have sent an extra copy of my letter to his principal seat in Wiltshire. Ah, here is the doctor now.'

'Well, doctor, how is your patient?' Lady Hermione asked.

'He sustained a knock on his head, presumably when he fell. More importantly he lost a lot of blood. The wound is satisfactory, and provided there is no infection, it should be healing by the end of the week.

'He will undoubtedly be thirsty when he awakes and I have told his valet to give him as much liquid as he wants. He is a strong, healthy young man and I see no reason why he should not make a full recovery. In the meantime, he needs to rest. I shall call again tomorrow.'

Anne starting breathing again. The news was as positive as they could have hoped for.

'Thank you, doctor,' Lady Hermione said. 'Anne, I think we should go home now and let Lord Peter sleep. We can come again tomorrow afternoon.'

As they stood in the entrance hall, putting on their hats and gloves, a thought struck Anne.

'Richards, is there a piano in the house?'

'Yes miss, there is, but it is covered up and has not been used for a long while.'

'Would you ask for it to be uncovered and cleaned, please? We will send a piano tuner to see if it needs adjustment.'

'Very good, miss,' Richards said, sounding a little puzzled.

On the way home, Lady Hermione asked Anne what she had in mind.

'I want to do something for Lord Peter, but the possibilities are rather limited. I can hardly spoon broth into his mouth, can I?

'However, once he is awake he will probably be bored if he is constrained to his bed, so I thought I could play the piano for him.'

'A excellent notion, my dear. I can see we will be coming here every day for the next week,' Hermione said dryly.

Precious Moments

'For goodness' sake, Anne, I am being exhausted by all your fidgeting!' Lady Hermione said.

'But, but ...' Anne said, waving her hands in the air as she was unable to find the right words.

'Mabel,' Lady Hermione said, 'go and find Miss Anne's outdoor things. She needs to take a walk around the garden to settle her nerves. Probably two or three circuits of the garden might be a good idea.'

'What if something has happened?'

'Everything has already happened. Well, nearly everything. But I don't think there is anything for you to be anxious about. Besides, if there was any cause for worry, they would have sent a message like yesterday, wouldn't they?

'Now go and get some fresh air and walk off some of your energy. If anyone comes from Ermcombe, I'll send for you.'

'Do you suppose we should have an early luncheon?'

Her aunt sighed. Anne was in such a hurry to go to Ermcombe.

'Very well, send Gerrard to me as you pass him.'

'And Aunt, shall we take Robbie with us?'

'Yes, yes, if you like; the dog and his lordship did seem to get along. However, Mabel should come too because they might not want the dog upstairs and she could mind him in the servants' hall.'

* * *

After a quick lunch, it wasn't long before they arrived at Ermcombe. Anne had been mentally urging the horses to go faster all the way there. As soon as the steps had been put down by a footman, she held her hand out for him to guide her down.

As she stepped on to the gravel she heard Robbie jump down beside her. She grabbed his handle and headed for the door. Mabel hurried to catch up and make sure she didn't trip on a step.

'Good afternoon, Miss Harford,' Richards said from the doorway.

'Richards, how is his lordship?' Anne asked, the moment she entered the house.

'The doctor is quite satisfied, miss, and my lord was awake and sitting up in bed a short while ago.'

'Oh, thank goodness,' Anne said, sagging slightly. 'Come, Robbie, let us go and see Lord Peter.'

Anne quickly headed for the stairs, followed by Mabel.

'Good afternoon, Lady Hermione,' Richards said in a calm, almost resigned, voice. 'May I take your bonnet and cloak?'

'You may,' she said, 'then you may conduct me to the breakfast-room and have tea sent up. I'm sure while I am waiting you can tell me about Lord Peter's progress.' She waved at the two girls and a dog going upstairs and sighed.

'These two ... three, should have

asked permission before racing upstairs, but Miss Anne has been in a fever of anxiety all morning. I suppose they can manage appropriately on their own.'

'Indeed, milady, I think we both understand the situation quite well. Andrew,' he said, turning to his other new footman, 'go to the kitchen and make a tea tray ready for Lady Hermione. While you are there, arrange for another to be sent up to his lordship's room.'

★ ★ ★

Peter had been dozing slightly, after drinking a bowl of beef broth, followed, at his insistence, by a couple of glasses of wine. The doctor had said to drink plenty of fluids, so Fredericks hadn't seen fit to argue with his master, especially since the wine would help him sleep.

Peter had woken at the sound of wheels on the gravel drive followed by distant voices. Now he waited to see who it was, while his valet straightened the bedclothes, propped him up with an extra pillow and placed a chair beside the bed.

Fredericks was clearly expecting the visitors to be coming upstairs to see his master. Peter hoped it would be Anne. Someone tapped on his bedroom door and Fredericks went to see who it was.

'Good afternoon, Miss Harford, Miss Mabel and, er . . . Robbie, I presume?'

Peter looked toward the door. He didn't really remember the details, but he had been told Anne had come the day before and had sat with him for a while.

It seemed she remembered the position of the bed as she came straight towards him. She held out a hand which he took and pressed to his lips. She blushed.

'How are you, my lord? I'm glad to know you are awake now,' she said quietly.

'I'm still very tired and have bit of a headache, but now you are here I am feeling much better. Please take the seat beside the bed and talk to me for a while.'

Anne felt for the chair, sat down and reached for his hand once more.

'I see you have brought Robbie with

you. I hope he got extra food as a reward for being instrumental in your rescue.'

'Yes, he did, but you are the one who should be getting the extra food because you're the one who actually rescued me, for which I will always be grateful.'

Peter chuckled.

'I'm hoping they'll give me some proper food later today. For now they're just giving me beef broth. Is Robbie allowed to put his feet on the bed so that I can stroke him?'

'Not really, but he is allowed to jump into my lap when my parents are not looking. Robbie, come, up!' she said, patting her knees.

'Robbie,' Peter said, 'you are a very good, very obedient dog.'

Just then a maid came in the open door with a tea tray and put it on a table in the corner.

'Robbie, get down,' Anne said, and he jumped back on to the floor.

Fredericks produced a small table which he placed next to Anne.

'Milord,' Mabel said, 'may I pour you

some tea?'

'Yes, thank you — also for you Miss Harford?' Peter said.

She nodded.

'You know, I should like it if you called me Anne, rather than Miss Harford. It seems unnecessarily formal after recent events.'

'Perhaps Miss Anne, then, as we wouldn't want to scandalise Lady Hermione, would we? And, in return, I would like it if you could call me Peter, at least as long as we are not in public.'

'I don't think she would mind. I do believe she has softened her opinion of you as you have done so much for us recently.'

Peter hoped it was the case. He also hoped to have an interview with Anne's father in the not too distant future and it would help if Lady Hermione was kindly disposed towards him now. Mabel placed a cup of tea at Anne's elbow and whispered to her. Anne carefully found the cup with her hand.

'Oh,' Anne said, pausing before she

picked it up, 'can you manage a cup of tea? They said you had been shot in the arm and it must be difficult to manage one-handed.'

'We're a sorry pair, aren't we? Struggling with the simple task of drinking tea. Never fear, Fredericks has put it where I can hold the saucer steady with my injured arm. My arm is in a sling, but the fingers still work.'

'You must guide me if you need help.'

Peter thought it would be good to have a few moments alone with Anne. In normal circumstances he would have invited her to walk in the garden or something, but this was out of the question at present.

'Fredericks, Robbie is a hero for showing us where to find Miss Anne, but it's his first time here. No doubt the staff below stairs would like to see him. Why don't you and Mabel take him down to meet them and see if Cook has any spare biscuits?

Fredericks and Mabel exchanged a long glance before Mabel called Robbie to her and they preceded Fredericks out of the room. They left the door open.

'They had better not be long and be back before my aunt comes to visit you,' Anne said, 'otherwise she really will be scandalised.'

'I understand she has written to both of our fathers about the smuggling incident.'

'Yes. I hope my father doesn't feel he needs to bring the whole family back. It would be very disappointing for my sister to be forced to abandon the season so soon.'

'How is she getting on? Does she write?'

'Yes, she is a frequent correspondent. She probably feels a little guilty I was left behind, although we both understand the reason why.

'Your parents were very obliging by introducing them around so they are not short of invitations. Sarah has even been granted a voucher for Almack's, so she is over the moon.'

'I'm glad. I did ask my father to help,

but I didn't know if he would be too busy. Perhaps he delegated the task to my mother, who I'm sure would be happy to have something to do.

'I don't have sisters so she will enjoy taking a girl around, showing them the right modistes and so forth. Hopefully your mother and Sarah are established already, because I won't be surprised if my mother turns up on the doorstep now she's heard I've been injured.'

'I hope she doesn't turn up too quickly, as then I doubt if I will be allowed up here to talk to you.'

'I hope to be allowed out of bed soon, so it need not be a problem. What is this I hear about a piano tuner coming and the maids polishing the piano?'

'Do you mind? I know it was a bit high-handed of me.'

'I don't mind at all. The prospect of you coming to entertain the invalid on the piano is delightful.'

They could hear footsteps and clicking paws returning down the corridor. Mabel and Fredericks came in, followed by Robbie. Robbie nudged Anne and she absent-mindedly rubbed his ears. They then heard more footsteps in the corridor and Lady Hermione appeared in the doorway with Richards standing behind her.

'Good afternoon, Lord Peter,' Lady Hermione said. 'I'm glad to hear you are on the mend, but I also hear you need to rest. I think it's time for Anne and myself to return home so that you may.'

'Thank you for coming to see me, my lady,' Peter said. 'I am hoping you will come back again tomorrow so Miss Anne may serenade me on the piano.'

Peter wondered briefly if 'serenade' had been a good choice of word. It did have romantic connotations and perhaps he should have said 'entertain'. He noticed the glimmer of a smile on Lady Hermione's lips and concluded it was not a problem. Maybe the dragon chaperone was damping her fire.

'I am sure we shall indeed see you again tomorrow.'

New Beginning

Lady Hermione was listening to Anne's piano playing when she heard a carriage arrive at the front of the house. Rising to her feet she went to the window. There was a post-chaise and four standing there with a footman letting down the steps. A gentleman descended whom she recognised as the Marquess of Morton.

'Lord Morton has arrived,' Lady Hermione said and Anne paused in her playing.

It seemed inevitable, Anne thought, that Peter's father or mother, or both, would come when they heard he had been injured. She had hoped it wouldn't be quite so soon. Would she be allowed to visit Peter after today?

The marquess could view with disfavour Anne and her aunt making frequent visits to what was, after all, his house. He might suppose Anne was trying to compromise his son into marriage and not want a blind girl as a daughter-in-law.

She sighed and her shoulders sagged.

Hermione then saw Richards hurry forwards to greet his lordship, who then turned back to the carriage and beckoned another person to step down as well. As he stepped down she saw it was Lord Harford.

'Oh — and your father is here, too,' Hermione said.

'Father? Are Mother and Sarah here?' Anne asked.

If they were, today's visit would probably be cut short as she would have to go home with them. She wanted to keep Peter to herself and not have her sister making up to him. Lady Hermione peered out of the window again.

'No. At least not yet. Why don't you resume playing for the moment?'

★   ★   ★

Peter had been lying in bed, listening to the music coming from the floor below. Tomorrow he intended to be out of bed and listening in the music room. In the meantime, he was daydreaming of how things could be before too long.

The house and estate was being slowly put back into order. The leakage of the estate coffers was ended, with the drainer in question probably near New England.

His father's first requirement had been to find out what was wrong at Ermcombe and he had done that. Father's second requirement had been to return it to profitability and this seemed achievable.

Now Peter had also put an end to smuggling here, this might make his father more positive, too. Before, he might have supposed Peter wild enough to join in with the smuggling, but now it was entirely clear this was not the case.

Would his father see how Peter had turned over a new leaf? Especially once Peter had explained he wanted to stay and make his home here, becoming a respectable landowner. He was no longer interested in kicking up a dust in London.

He had to persuade his father to grant

him the estate and the sooner, the better. If his father did so, Peter could make an offer to a certain young pianist who was currently entertaining him.

Would Peter's father object to him marrying a blind girl? Peter could see no reason why he should. Peter wasn't even the spare, never mind the heir, and there would be no reason for embarrassment when they visited London. They definitely needed to visit London, because he had every intention of waltzing with Anne at Almack's.

Would Anne's father refuse? Again, Peter didn't see why he should, provided Harford could be convinced Peter could support his daughter. It would surely be reassuring for the Harfords to have Anne living next door, in an area familiar to her and in a place very convenient for her parents to visit.

The music suddenly stopped and Fredericks looked up from mending a bullet hole in a shirt. There were faint sounds coming from outside and Fredericks went to the window.

'Lord Morton has arrived, sir,' Fredericks said.

'He hasn't wasted any time, has he?'

Peter was not surprised his father had come, and he had been hoping he would come soon anyway. He wanted to convince his father to make the estate over to him before the end of the quarter.

'No, sir, he has come in a post-chaise and four, so must have been in a hurry to get here.'

'Is my mother with him?'

'Ah . . . no sir, no, it's not the marchioness, it's Baron Harford.'

'Harford? Not surprising, I suppose, after his daughter was kidnapped.'

The only surprising thing was how both fathers had come together. He wondered exactly how much detail Lady Hermione had put in her letters.

Was Harford here to tell him to keep his distance? After all, Lady Hermione had given Harford a pretty damning view of Peter's morals and behaviour before the Harfords had gone off to London.

As far as Peter was aware, their fathers would have been barely acquainted, so he wondered what they had spoken about on their journey.

Fredericks bustled about, making everything tidy.

★ ★ ★

The door to the music room opened and Lady Hermione put a hand on Anne's shoulder so she knew to stop playing and stand to greet the gentlemen.

'Lady Hermione, it is a pleasure to see you again,' Lord Morton said in a friendly tone of voice as he bowed to them. 'And this young lady is, I suppose, Miss Anne Harford.'

Anne curtseyed.

'My compliments on your playing, it sounded impressive,' he continued. 'I look forward to hearing more in due course. In the meantime I must go up to see my son.' He nodded to them both and left the room.

Baron Harford stepped further into

the room and kissed Lady Hermione's cheek before doing the same to Anne. A maid carrying a tray of coffee had followed him in.

'It seems there have been some dramatic events while we have been away. Come and join me in some coffee while you tell me all about it.' He took Anne's hand and drew her forward to a sofa while Hermione attended to the coffee.

'Anne,' he said softly, 'are you well? Are you very shaken by your experience? You could go back with me to London if you would rather be with your mother.'

What? No! Anne thought. She absolutely, definitely, did not want to go to London. Not now. No, she liked being exactly where she was at the moment and would have to persuade him to leave her here. If her mother and Sarah weren't already on their way home, she should convince her father to keep them in London.

'Oh, no, Father, it was very frightening at the time but the danger has passed. The soldiers took the smugglers away, so they won't be troubling us again.

'I am quite comfortable here and I enjoy Aunt Hermione's company. Aunt Hermione, you don't mind if we stay here, do you?'

'Oh, no, certainly not. My stay here has been . . . eventful and, and . . . full of interest, I'm in no hurry to go home. I think we should stay here.

'Sarah and her mother should stay in London for the rest of the season, too. If they were to leave so soon it would give the wrong impression entirely.'

Anne wanted to hug her aunt for saying exactly the right thing. She wasn't sure what her aunt's reaction would be if she was hugged. However, she suspected her aunt had a warmer heart than she liked to show to the rest of the world.

'Very well,' Harford said, 'I shall go and speak to Lord Peter once his father has seen him. Then we should go home, I'm quite exhausted by the hurried journey from London. Do you have the landau here?'

'Yes, we do, so you can send the post-chaise away unless Lord Morton needs it.'

'I think he plans to stay for a few days and his travelling coach with our valets should turn up some time tomorrow, so he won't need it. I'll tell the butler. What's his name?'

'It's Mr Richards, Papa.'

'Good. Now where is the bell rope?'

* * *

The marquess strode into Peter's bed-chamber. Fredericks bowed to him before disappearing into the dressing-room.

'Peter! How are you, my boy?' He surveyed Peter's sling. 'Ball in the shoulder?'

'No, sir, ball in the arm, but it went all the way through, so at least the surgeon didn't have to dig it out of me. It hurt like the devil, but seems to be easing now, so I hope to be allowed out of bed tomorrow.'

'You got the other fellow, I hear.'

'Yes; lucky shot, really. It was pretty dark and I barely remember pulling the

228

trigger, so it was pure chance I was pointing the pistol in the right direction.'

'More likely the time you spent practising at Manton's was well spent and you did it instinctively.'

'Perhaps. In any case, he won't be standing trial and the rest of them can blame him for pressuring them into smuggling.'

'I doubt this will carry much weight with the magistrates.'

'No,' Peter said, 'but it could be the difference between hanging and transportation.'

'You have sympathy for them?'

Peter saw he didn't want his father to think he approved of smuggling, when he wanted his father to help him.

'No. They knew the risk they were taking. I might have a little sympathy for families left behind who might end up in the workhouse, but this is all. At least the farmhands did what they were told and kept away from the smuggling gang.'

'Some of our farmers were involved?'

'Farmhands. Extra labour and they

needed the money it produced. After I cut the farm rents back to where they belonged, they co-operated. They realised, too, it wasn't you or me who had raised their rents but Smith, the steward.

'It was clever of Smith to squeeze the farmers so then they needed the extra income from smuggling. He, of course, blamed you for the high rents.'

'You haven't said so, but I realise a lot of it was my fault. I should have sent someone to inspect the place a long time ago or else come myself to take a look. I've been too busy in government with the war against Napoleon to give it the attention it deserved.'

Peter sensed his father was feeling guilty, not just about the mismanagement and permitted smuggling, but indirectly for Peter's injuries. He thought it might be the moment to press his advantage.

'Of course, there is still much to be done. The estate and the farmers have been short of cash, so there are a lot of repairs and necessary improvements which haven't been done. Even with the rent reduction there is a suggestion the harvest will be poor this year.

'If it proves to be the case, it may be difficult to make the estate profitable by the end of the quarter, however hard I and the farmers work. I'm hoping you will be indulgent about making the estate over to me at the end of the quarter nonetheless.'

His father studied Peter for several long minutes while Peter held his breath.

'Are you planning then to become a farmer?'

'Well, not exactly a farmer, but there is plenty to do on the estate, besides the tenant farms. As well, my new stable master is a farrier, ex Royal Horse Guards, so I plan to install a small forge beside the stables.

'Not too close of course, due to the fire risk, but once it is set up he can shoe all the horses on the estate and make farm tools as well. I'm hoping it might even make a small profit beyond saving us some costs.'

Peter paused as he realised he was

sounding enthusiastic about something which might never come to pass if the estate didn't become his. His father was regarding him with a raised eyebrow.

'Well,' the marquess said, 'we shall see. Tomorrow I shall ride around with young Baines to have a look for myself. As for now, I hardly slept on the way down here. We only stopped for a few hours between the moon setting and the sun rising.

'I am going to have an early night, so I will see you tomorrow. I'll send up Harford before he goes home. He wants to thank you for rescuing his daughter. Excellent pianist, by the way.'

Well, Peter thought, this conversation was a lot better than the last time we met.

His father hadn't agreed to give him Ermcombe yet, but he hadn't dismissed it, either. Interesting as well, that he never queried why Lady Hermione and Anne were here.

A few minutes later, Fredericks opened the door to Baron Harford.

'Lord Peter, I want to thank you for

rescuing Anne from those smugglers. She and my aunt have been telling me all about it.'

'Ah, well, you could say it was my fault in the first place she was abducted. If I hadn't resisted the smuggling gang, it wouldn't have happened at all, so it was more a case of making amends.'

'Perhaps, but I gather you have been keeping them company anyway, which was good of you. We were a little worried at the necessity of leaving Anne behind with only my aunt to keep her company.

'I offered to take her with me back to London, but they were both most insistent they wanted to stay here. I understand Anne has volunteered to entertain you on the piano while you are recuperating, so we will all be returning again tomorrow. If you are too busy with your father, you must let us know and we'll go home so we don't get in your way.'

'I'm sure it won't be a problem and I look forward to seeing you tomorrow,' Peter said as they shook hands.

The following morning the doctor declared himself satisfied. Peter could get out of bed, but was to stay at home for a few days until the doctor called again.

Now Peter was sitting in a chair whilst Fredericks very carefully threaded a shirt sleeve over Peter's arm and bandage. Peter was gritting his teeth as his upper arm was still painful.

'Will my jacket fit?' he asked.

'I suggest you wear your riding jacket sir, it is more roomy. When it is on, I shall replace your sling, arrange a neckcloth and you will be fit to be seen.'

Once he was dressed, Fredericks steadied Peter as he made his way down to the breakfast-room for lunch.

'Following your comments about the food at the Mayflower Inn, sir,' Richards said, 'and your wish for some 'proper food' as you put it, Cook has taken the liberty of making some Cornish pasties. She thought they might be convenient to eat with only one hand.'

'Ah ,yes, excellent. Thank Cook for me if you will,' Peter said as Richards poured him a glass of wine. Just then Lord Morton arrived in the breakfast-room.

'Excellent, you're up and about,' he said to Peter, then pointed to the pasties. 'What are these?'

'They are a hearty local dish called Cornish pasties. Just the thing when you're been out riding,' Peter said with a grin.

'Good, it has given me an appetite and I have seen what you said about repairs and so forth on the estate.'

Richards beckoned to the footman and they left the room, closing the door behind themselves.

'Now,' Peter's father said, 'about the estate. How do I know you won't just sell the place and head back to London?'

'I'm intending to settle down here, marry and raise a family. To do so I need somewhere to live and an income. Ermcombe would suit me very well.'

'Marry, eh? Am I to suppose you

mean Harford's eldest?'

'Exactly so, but I can't make her an offer if I can't support her.'

'She's blind. How would you manage? Does blindness run in the family?'

'We already manage pretty well. She has an intelligent maid and a clever guide dog. She's blind because she had measles when she was a baby.'

Lord Morton sat back in his chair and drummed his fingers on the table.

'Very well, provided Harford gives his consent and the girl accepts you, the estate will be yours as a wedding gift.'

'Thank you, Father,' Peter said and he reached across the table to grip his father's hand.

'Your mother will be here soon, so the housekeeper and maids had better bustle about. Your mother will have a poor opinion of all the dust and Holland covers.'

'Excuse me, my lords, but the party from Harford House has arrived,' Richards said as they were finishing their coffee.

'Conduct the ladies to the music room

if you please,' Lord Morton said, 'and I will join them. Ask Lord Harford to step in here for a moment as Lord Peter wishes a word with him.'

Peter nodded at his father, who stood to follow Richards.

A couple of minutes later, the baron came into the room and Peter rose.

'I'm glad to see you looking better, Lord Peter. How may I help you?'

'My father has just agreed to give me the Ermcombe estate for my own. I have told him I intend to remain here and make it my home. As I am now in a position to support a wife and family I would like your permission to pay my addresses to Miss Anne.'

'Oh. Well,' the baron said, 'I see. You don't mind she is blind?'

Why on earth do people keep saying this, Peter thought. If he minded he wouldn't be asking, would he?

He wanted to marry her because he was in love with her. But it was not the moment to become impatient with his future father-in-law.

'No, sir. I regard her with deep affection and I believe the sentiment is returned.'

'Frankly, I don't know you very well, but it seems my aunt has revised her opinion and now approves of you.

'I have also got to know your father on our journey down here and I have the idea he has also been revising his view, too. So, yes, you have my leave to speak to her.'

'Thank you. Shall we go to the music room? Then perhaps you can ask Lady Hermione to go with you and my father to inspect the gardens.

'No doubt she will see what needs to be done and will be able to advise me.'

'The gardens? Oh, yes, I see. I'm sure her advice will be invaluable.'

They entered the room to find Lord Morton chatting with Lady Hermione while Anne played a quiet air.

'Aunt Hermione,' the baron said, 'Lord Peter has asked us to go with Lord Morton to take a look at the gardens.'

Lady Hermione and Anne both rose,

and Hermione went to offer a hand to Anne.

'I'm sure Anne would prefer to remain here. Lord Peter will keep her company,' the baron said.

Hermione turned to her nephew, with a raised eyebrow, but he just nodded emphatically. Her eyes suddenly widened with understanding.

Lord Morton grinned at her and waved them both out of the room, closing the door behind them.

Peter went to the piano and gently took her hand.

'Anne, they have left us alone as there is something particular I want to ask you. When I was told you had been abducted, it struck fear into my heart and I could think of nothing other than going to find you, the girl I loved.

'My father has given me the Ermcombe estate for my own and there is nothing I would like better than to bring you here as my bride.

'Anne, will you do me the honour of becoming my wife?'